WITHDRAWN

INVALUABLE

TRIDENT CODE #2

ALANA ALBERTSON

Invaluable
Book Two in THE TRIDENT CODE
Copyright © 2017 by Alana Albertson
Cover design by Regina Wamba of MaeIDesign.com
Cover Models: Alli Lashley and Maurice Mooney

Bolero Books, LLC
11956 Bernardo Plaza Dr. #510
San Diego, CA 92128
www.bolerobooks.com

ISBN-13: 978-1-941665-77-0
All rights reserved.

Without limiting the rights under copyright reserved above, no part of this publication may be reproduced, stored in or introduced into a retrieval system, or transmitted, in any form, or by any means (electronic, mechanical, photocopying, recording, or otherwise) without the prior written permission of both the copyright owner and the above publisher of this book.
This is a work of fiction. Names, characters, places, brands, media, and incidents are either the product of the author's imagination or are used fictitiously. The author acknowledges the trademarked status and trademark owners of various products, bands, and/or restaurants referenced in this work of fiction, which have been used without permission. The publication/use of these trademarks is not authorized, associated with, or sponsored by the trademark owners.

Created with Vellum

Individuals play the game, but Teams beat the odds.

— SEAL Team Saying

INVALUABLE

I'll be honest with you—I'm no saint. Sure, I turned down my 9.6-million-dollar football contract to join the Teams but I'll never tell you the real reason why. The media has anointed me a selfless, patriotic American hero. But it isn't that deep—I just want some action.

A one-night stand with a San Diego coed. I picked her out of a steamy nightclub—sexy blonde hair, full breasts, nice ass. I savored her warm touch, the scent of her perfume, and the sound of her laughter. After she rode me all night, I took in the ocean view from my condo, thankful for the blissful memories she gave me to get me through my long deployment.

I cross paths with Miss San Diego again halfway across the world in Afghanistan. Turns out she is a professional cheerleader on a patriotic tour sent to entertain my Team.

I gaze into her beautiful blue eyes and give her my word that she's safe with me. And my word is my bond.

Then she is kidnapped.

Whoever took her, took the wrong girl. Because I will tear this country apart to find her.

I'll never win MVP, never get a championship ring, but **some heroes don't play games.**

1

KYLE

LATE SUMMER, SAN DIEGO

Summertime in San Diego brought out all of the honeys, and the blonde doll swaying her body to the latest jam was no exception. There was something about the way she held herself that set her apart from the typical. women of San Diego. She danced on a platform while the fluorescent lights highlighted her glistening, sand-colored golden skin. I bit my lip. Man, she was fine. Her hips swirled around, and I couldn't help but imagine them swiveling on top of me. She wore a tight, white tank top with a turquoise bikini top peeking through and a bubblegum-pink skirt that hit right at her juicy thighs—I wouldn't be satisfied until I saw her clothes strewn all over my floor.

I glanced at the window to see a long line of people waiting outside, hopeful to get into Green Flash Bar & Grill, Pacific Beach's hottest nightclub. This place was always hopping, especially on Taco Tuesday. It was walking distance to the beach, had a DJ spinning dance tracks, and cheap beer and great food. I scanned the place again. Always aware of my surroundings, I also noted the green neon lights of the exits in case I needed to make a hasty escape.

My wingman for the night, Victor Gonzales, nursed his beer. He normally wasn't my first choice for a sidekick, but my best buddy Patrick Walsh had ditched me for his new chick, Annie, who we'd rescued. It was a fresh relationship, yet more intense than most. Poor girl had been kidnapped during spring break in the Caribbean and forced into sex slavery. But no small-time sex-ring scared us. We were motherfucking United States Navy SEALs. There was never a question—we had to save her. Now she was safe back home in San Diego, madly in love with her savior, Pat. It was like the plot of a Hollywood movie. Despite swearing to us he wasn't interested in a relationship with her, that he was only doing his job, Pat was acting like a lovesick puppy, too. Don't get me wrong, I was happy for the dude, but I missed my bro. And it was hard to understand how he could be satisfied with carrying on with a relationship with our lifestyle.

At least Vic had game—boy could dance. The women went crazy over his shiny black hair, deep dimples, and tattooed arms. And he understood my logic. So that was a plus. There were no real feelings involved so no one got hurt. Just over the surface was a safe place to be. Pat normally hung out at the bar all night, drinking himself into oblivion. At least now he appeared sated. A warm body did a hell of a lot more than reaching the bottom of a bottle, that was for sure. So I couldn't knock him.

Vic and I sat in silence after we had just devoured a plate of tacos. They were good, but not as delicious as the ones Vic's mom made. Vic was on his third Corona. I took a swig of my own beer and stared intently back at blondie. Would she smile when she caught me undressing her with my eyes? Or would she roll hers and spin away from me? I would put money on the former. I wasn't a conceited prick all the time, but it was safe to say I didn't have any problems with the ladies. At six-foot-five, I towered over the other men at this club. Height had its advantages. The bars in this coastal party town were packed with frat boys, surfers, Marines, and sailors. But I stood out. I wasn't just your average sailor—I was a Navy SEAL and a former professional linebacker, with broad shoulders and solid muscles that resembled a brick wall. I'd left behind money and fame to make a difference in the world, do something I believed in far more than the game. Something I'd die for. It was a personal decision. One I was proud of.

Blondie made strong eye contact with me and then ducked her head away. Just as I thought—she wanted me. I could never tell if these chicks wanted to date a brother, especially one who was as intimidating to look at as I was. Sure, everyone tried to pretend we were race blind ever since our country had elected a black president, but as one of only a handful of African-American Navy SEALs, I was reminded every day I stood out.

I shouted to Vic, "I'm going in. You want her friend?" Blondie's girlfriend had long, straight, dark hair that touched her ass. Petite, round booty and a nice rack. Just his type.

Vic nodded and we set our beers down and followed the bass-filled path up to the platform. The ground thumped with vibrations. No words. I started grooving behind Barbie. If the way she had looked at me was any indication, she wasn't tight-laced. And I was open to any and all possibilities that got me close to her body. She shrugged her shoulders and gave me a coy smile. I was in. I wrapped my arms around her and felt her tight little ass grind up against my cock. Life was good. Inhibition was nowhere to be seen.

Blondie smelled salty and sweet, sandy even, like she'd just spent the day at the beach. And the sensual way she moved made me certain she was a dancer. I just hoped she wasn't the type who earned her living on the pole. Then I'd know I didn't inspire her, it was merely her occupation. "What's your name, sweetheart?" I whispered in her ear so she could hear me over the music.

"I'm Sara," she shouted back. She nodded to her friend. "And this is Maya."

"Nice to meet you, Sara. I'm Kyle. And this is my buddy, Vic. Can we buy you ladies some drinks?"

Her head bobbed with the music, not fully committing to a yes, but she followed me off the platform. Always in control, I took her hand, and we found a table near the bar, where I signaled to the cocktail waitress to take our order. She would be over in a second. We were regulars, and she knew we were huge tippers.

I glanced at her friend Maya, who clearly wanted to be somewhere else. She wasn't even making eye contact with Vic or me. I studied her closely, taking note of her massive diamond earrings, tiny designer purse, and red-soled heels which were visible when she crossed her legs. The girl was either loaded or looking for a sugar daddy. I'd been wrong—she definitely wasn't a good match for Vic.

Sara, on the other hand, sported a small, gold necklace shaped like the Lone Star state, an iPhone case with slots for her ID and a few credit cards, and wore flip-flops adorned with rhinestones. I felt my pulse steady—it was refreshing to meet a girl who didn't appear to be materialistic. Being into labels and appearing money-orientated was the quickest way to lose my interest.

The waitress came over and Vic and I ordered two beers, Sara wanted a Malibu and Coke, and her friend Maya just asked for a glass of water. Probably because she was waiting to be offered some thousand-dollar glass of champagne. Nope. Vic definitely wasn't getting any tonight.

I turned my attention to Sara. Her blonde hair was cut in one of those crisp bobs, revealing her delicate neck. Her tits looked real, a rarity in Southern California. "So, Sara, what do you do for a living?"

"I go to SDSU, getting my degree in education. Right now, I work part-time at a preschool. How about you?"

Hot for teacher. Sounded good to me. Refreshing compared to the typical answers from many of the local girls I'd met here. Most had dreams of becoming a model, Instagram star, or reality show wannabe. And with her looks, if she wanted that life, she could easily get it.

"I play football."

Her face brightened. "I love football. I grew up a huge Dallas Wranglers fan, but I also love the San Diego Wildfires."

She was refreshing to talk to—I loved a woman who loved sports. "I guess we have the love of the sport in common." I paused. For a moment I wanted to tell her the truth. But I never told anyone the real reason I'd quit football and joined the Teams.

Not my friends, nor my family.

Not even my Team.

And I made it a habit to never tell anyone my current job. Even if it was guaranteed to get me pussy.

"It doesn't matter what you do as long as you're happy. That's my motto."

I dug her northern Texas accent. Most girls started asking a ton of questions once I mentioned pro ball, but not Sara. Maybe she didn't care about my money and actually wanted to get to know me. That would be nice for a change. I was going to find out if she was bluffing.

The waitress brought us our drinks. A new song began. The music boomed, and I could barely hear a word of what Sara said from there on out. Vic tried to talk to Maya but neither of them seemed all that interested. That shit was brutal to watch. And I wasn't into audiences. It was time to make my move.

I lightly brushed Sara's hair off her face, letting my hand linger at the nape of her neck. "It's too loud in here. Tell you what—I live down the street. You want to go back to my place? Hang out there for a while?" I smiled. I definitely had balls.

She blinked rapidly and crossed her arms. For a second I thought she'd decline. She looked at the disaster happening to her right then back at me. "I'd love to," she said under her breath.

Well I'll be damned.

Sara hugged her friend and whispered something in her ear. Maya squinted, and her face showed a disapproving scowl.

I signaled to Vic to help a brother out. Poor dude had to take one for the team.

Vic turned to Maya, "I'll give you a ride home."

Maya gave a reluctant nod, and we said our good-byes. I found it funny she'd judge her friend at the drop of a hat for going home with a complete stranger, but had no issues with getting a ride from one. Unreal. But she wasn't my problem. I put my arm around Sara and led her out of the bar past the bouncers. A gentle breeze from the ocean was a welcome change from the stale air and sweat from the club. The neon lights of the other marquees glowed in the distance as we walked toward the beach.

It always boggled my mind a girl would honestly go home with a man whom she'd just met in a club, especially knowing what had happened to Annie, but I wasn't complaining. And let's face it, Sara was safer with me than she would be with any other man, though there was absolutely no way she could be certain I wasn't a serial killer or rapist.

I hadn't had a full conversation with this chick and didn't even know her last name, but it didn't matter—this was going to be a one-night stand. I was only in town for the next month before I deployed again, but she didn't need to know that.

All she needed to know was I thought she was the sexiest girl in the club, and I planned to ravage every inch of her body tonight.

2

SARA

What had I been thinking? Was I seriously going home with a man who I had just met? We walked quietly down the crowded sidewalk, his hand wrapped around mine, and he smiled. Underneath that easy smile, I knew he must've thought I was so easy, but I swear I had never done this before. Ever. I didn't bother to utter those words. They were so clichéd, even if they were the truth.

I couldn't explain it. I was drawn to him. Lord, he was sexy. He was well over six feet, with bulging muscles and smooth skin the color of my grandmother's antique mahogany armoire, his kind, intense brown eyes being the most striking. There was a familiarity about him I couldn't explain. I could've sworn I'd seen him before—and when I remembered he'd said he was a football player, it clicked. I was almost sure I'd seen him making a play on the field when I had watched a Wranglers game with my brothers. But I wasn't one to spend game day checking out the players. Every time I went to a football game, my eyes focused on the cheerleaders. They were so beautiful, bright, and vivacious. Everything I wasn't. I'd been an awkward teen, a loner, and had battled depression after my dad had left us. The only solace I'd found was practicing dance daily until my feet bled. If only I worked harder, turned faster, and stretched more, I too could one day be on that field.

And now I was a rookie San Diego Wildfire Girl; a newbie Spark.

Not that I told Kyle I was a cheerleader—I never mentioned it to guys I met. The minute a man knew I was on a pro dance squad, he would react in one of three ways. One—I was a conquest, a trophy to fuck and then forget about. Two—I was a bimbo, some whore who danced in short shorts, clearly incapable of any meaningful conversation. Or three—I was a diva, and somehow instantly way out of his league. The fanboying started, quickly followed by the, "Can you get me free tickets?" or, "Come on, babe, help me meet my favorite player," pleas. So no, just no. I kept my secret to myself. Sure, the occasional guy recognized me from my newly released Miss September calendar picture, which said dude probably jerked off to, but this was my first season and there were so many blondes in San Diego, I seemed to blend in well.

Now Kyle, he was different. I knew he was a football player. But I also knew he didn't play for the Wildfires. Ha, I had to memorize the names and positions of every member of the team for auditions. No way was I going to tell him I shook my pom-poms for a possible rival team. He'd think I lacked team loyalty. And as was the case with many cheerleaders, he'd think I was a gold digger and a jersey chaser. Most players figured that we women became cheerleaders to hook up with and be maintained by the guys on the team. That simply was not true. Besides my love for dancing, the real reason I became a cheerleader was for all the great opportunities to do charity work. Even though the season had just begun, we'd already done fundraisers for breast cancer, military families, shelter pets, and foster kids.

I also loved that we were role models to little girls. All the ladies on our squad were either in college, had degrees, or worked full time. Our group included doctors, lawyers, teachers, and even scientists. I was proud to be part of such a strong sisterhood. But I wanted to get to know Kyle first before I explained all of this to him. So I would keep my mouth shut, well at least outside of the bedroom.

Besides the occasional quick stops to admire the faraway waves crashing on the shore, we walked down the busy boardwalk that lined the beach. Now Kyle's strong arm was wrapped around my shoulders and the heat from his body filled mine. I should've been scared; I mean, he could've been a sociopath. But I felt safe, protected.

He led me into an alleyway between two garages that led to a stone path. I held my breath but it wasn't because I was nervous. I was impressed. His house was right on the beach. This man had to be loaded. The thought crossed my mind—did he think I was interested in him because of his money? No. I couldn't think like that. I'd agreed to go home with him before I'd seen his home. I was interested in him. And only him.

He opened the door and I found myself standing in a huge glass atrium, to my left a serene koi pond under the stairs, above me a retractable roof with views of the stars. The furniture was very modern, masculine, and sleek: steel-gray sofa, shiny black coffee table, monster flat-screen TV above the stone fireplace. He had incredible taste. I'd give him that.

"Sara, can I get you something to drink?"

"Water would be great. Thanks." He smirked at my choice of drink and I felt the need to give an acceptable explanation. "I'm feeling a bit dehydrated." The truth was I didn't need any more alcohol; I wanted to be in control. I wanted to remember this night.

He nodded, opening two mini bottles of chilled water, and poured them into two glasses at the bar, handing me one. We drank our water, and I glanced around his place. I wasn't exactly sure what had possessed me to go home with this man. I rarely indulged in down time. Last year, I'd spent every second of free time I'd had training for auditions. Dancing, working out, dieting, preparing to make the team had become my life. Over four hundred girls tried out for one of the coveted twenty-eight spots, but veterans always took most of those positions. Only eleven rookies were selected and hearing our director call my name had been like an out-of-body experience. Even better, I was the only rookie chosen for show group—which meant I'd get to travel and perform for our troops overseas during this holiday season. It was such an honor.

But I'd completely put my life on hold to achieve my goal. For an entire year, I didn't party or hook up with any guys at all. When the season finally started, preparing for our swimsuit shoot took over my life. It finally happened last week in Mexico, so I figured I deserved to cut loose. Maya and I had spent the entire day at the beach, and then we hit the clubs. Some saw it odd that my best friend was the captain, but we didn't see positions, just friendship. Once we'd entered the club, other guys had talked to me, some had even tried to pick me up, but I hadn't been interested at all—until Kyle.

But I didn't know this guy. Second-guessing reared its ugly head. If something happened to me, no one would know where to look for me. All Maya knew was I'd went home with a guy named Kyle. Maybe I should text her.

Before I could reach for my phone, Kyle placed his hand on my back. "So, where are you from, sweetheart?"

I pointed to my necklace. "Dallas. I love it there—can't wait to move back home. But I always wanted to live near the beach."

"I love Dallas. Greatest people out there. Warm, hardworking, patriotic, many of them deeply religious."

He paused over the word religious. As a cheerleader, I'd been through strict media training—never talk about politics or religion. But let's be honest, this was a one night stand not a media interview. Besides, something about Kyle's presence made me break yet another rule. He was getting really good at that.

"Yeah, that's totally true. Everyone back home is so friendly. I really miss that. I know this is a military town and all, but I felt a stronger connection back in Texas. I come from a family of Marines. My father is a former Marine, and so are my two brothers." I swallowed and pushed the heartache out of my head. I refused to mention how my father had abandoned his family, destroying our happiness when we found out he led a secret double life.

His lips widened into a smile. "No kidding. My father was a Devil Dawg, too. So you know what it's like to be raised in a strict household. Man, my father didn't let me get away with anything."

I relaxed back into the sofa, gazing up at the stars above. I didn't want to think of what we did or didn't get away with. All I thought about was what my father had gotten away with for so long, right under our noses. Nonetheless, it would be rude not to answer his question. There was this ease between us, and I was pleasantly surprised we had something in common besides the intense sexual attraction. I transported myself back to a happier time. The time before we'd been left. "Yup. My dad didn't let me date until I was sixteen. He would clean his guns when my boyfriends would come by." I smiled at the memory.

Kyle let out a deep laugh. "Sounds like my type of guy. He knew he had something precious." The smile fell from my lips and he must have interpreted it as me growing serious; taking the conversation to the next level. His eyes started slowing undressing me, and I felt the tone in the room change. His eyes hooded when he said, "Let me show you something. Upstairs."

Right then, some women may have become nervous. But I

wasn't shy; I knew why I'd come here tonight. I wanted him, and he wanted me.

He took my hand, and we walked upstairs to his bedroom. It was beautiful. Crisp white sheets and duvet on a plush dark-framed bed. Two end tables that held books, coasters, and small lamps. Across from the bed, a large flat-screen TV hung on the wall. A tall, dark dresser beneath it. Simple and elegant. Like he barely slept there. But he didn't stop near the king-sized bed—he continued past glass doors out onto the deck, a Jacuzzi beckoning us under the stars. Smooth.

I caught his gaze, and pulled my tank top off, wiggling out of my skirt and revealing my bikini underneath. Kyle gave me a full-body eye fuck, and peeled off his own shirt, as if he was challenging me.

And holy lord, he won the body contest, hands down. I'd never seen a body that ripped up close. Was that an eight-pack? His abs were so defined it was as if they were drawn in. Though I was sure he appreciated my soft curves just as much as I was enjoying the definition in his. His arms were massive, putting most guys to shame. I couldn't stop staring, and my mouth opened a tad.

Before I could speak, he switched the spa on, disappeared into his bedroom, and emerged a few moments later in light blue swim trunks. They hung low on his hips. "Ladies first."

I slipped into the bubbles, the jets massaging my legs. My calves and back were killing me from a long week of cheer practice. Our director was a total witch, demanding we dedicate our lives to the squad. She weighed us before every practice, even when we were on that time of the month. Heaven forbid if we gained a pound, we wouldn't be allowed to cheer in that week's game. The flat stomach. The demanding diet. Prim and proper at all times. It was all complete torture. If she saw me now, she'd freak! Going home with some random guy I'd just met. Her words echoed in my head, "Sara, you are a Wildfire Girl twenty-four hours a day. Whether you're in uniform or not." Well I was definitely not in my uniform at the moment; I was half naked with a hotter-than-sin man.

Kyle climbed into the hot tub, and pulled me back, close to him. We semi floated, and I lay against his firm chest as we spoke. The conversation was easy and relaxed. He felt amazing, and goose bumps ran down my arms and back.

"This place is incredible. I can't believe you live right on the beach. You're very fortunate."

"Well, don't get too impressed, doll. I own it with two buddies of mine. We bought it as an investment a few years back. But they live up north during the season, so it's all mine for now."

An investment. I liked this guy more and more. Even in just the six months I'd made the squad, I'd seen it all with football players—blowing all their money on cars, houses, drugs, and women.

The conversation continued at a comfortable pace, a part of each of our bodies always touching. He massaged my neck and shoulders then glided his hands down my arms as I touched his legs. He was solid. And I felt cocooned in more than muscle. He was nothing like I thought. As the conversation continued, I saw there was more to him than met the eye. I gasped when he ran his lips across my ear. Then he nipped the sensitive shell. Firecrackers went off inside me in response. Water sloshed as I twisted, and sat face to face with him. The hot water warmed my skin, but Kyle's words warmed my soul. My gut told me he was for real, he wasn't just playing me, we had an actual connection. Maybe this wasn't just a one-night stand. I considered confessing my own football secret to him, but just as my lips opened, Kyle cupped my face with one large hand and kissed me.

Oh, this man. I almost melted and became one with the water. The coarse hair on his face tickled when it grazed my chin, his full lips pressed against me, his warm, inviting tongue invaded my mouth and stroked with mine. His free hand grasped at my thigh, while the other held me in place, his kisses becoming more urgent. My body began to tingle. And I attempted to kiss him back with the same passion but he was completely in control. That hold never wavered. He had me just where he wanted me. He controlled the show.

These kisses weren't sweet. No, they were laced with firmness and all-consuming lust. I'd never been kissed like this before. He was all man. And all mine, if only for the night.

My fingers dug into his strong shoulders, the water glistening off his back, shining against the night sky. I grinded against him, moaning louder the harder he kissed me. My clit hummed as I rubbed on the outline of his impressive length. His cock twitched through the fabric against my stomach, and I gyrated harder till our clothes were just a formality. The way my skin pressed to his, they might as well have been nonexistent.

He let out a growl, like a hungry animal. "Out of the water." I squeaked when he lifted me, propping me on the edge of the Jacuzzi, and parted my thighs. I was exposed under the stars for any beach stroller to see.

And I didn't care. All I was concerned about was the pang in my core, the ache, the need for him to fill me up. Little did I know, I'd be waiting. The difference in temperature made my nipples harden. He stood, hovering over me, and blocked any potential view from behind him. "How wet are you, Sara?" His sight homed in on the small triangle covering my center, and I almost clinched my legs shut. His eyes smoldered as he waited for my reply. And I grew wetter the longer he stared. I wanted him to touch me. I leaned back the best I could, holding myself up with my palms, and held his stare.

"Very," I practically purred.

"Let me see."

"You want me to undress? Right here?" I asked, a bit panicked, but way turned on.

"Just the bottoms, sweetheart. Take them off and part your lips. Let me see how wet I make you." My chest thundered as I straightened, my legs dropping into the water, and brought my hands to my hips, and undid the bows holding the swimsuit in place. As soon as it fell to the edge of the tub, the night breeze caressed my sensitive flesh. Wet legs propped back on the ledge, I opened them, bringing a hand to my middle. I parted my lips and ran two fingers down the middle, letting them sink in when I reached the bottom. Then I presented the lubricated fingers to him.

"Fuck." He groaned, the water splashing as he squatted.

"Come here, baby. I'm gonna lick you until you come all over my face." Those words alone almost made me lose it. I arched my back, and spread my legs more. He undid my bikini top and kissed each of my nipples. Taking hold of my bottom, he cupped my ass and brought my pussy to his face. "Pretty. Pink. Perfect." His deep voice excited me. My pussy pulsed when he leaned in and took a whiff of my most intimate area. "Even your scent is perfect," he uttered before he buried his face into my pussy.

I gasped as Kyle devoured me. He grunted as he took long lap after lap of my pussy. And I thought I'd blacken out from every slow death of sensation. The stubble on his face tickled my thighs, and his tongue lapped deeply at my opening, sending me into a frenzy. I was no virgin, but I honest to God had never had a man make me feel so much so fast. My ex-boyfriend had always been too sweet, too gentle, when I truly wanted it hard and rough. My other hookups had been so awkward, filled with regret or drunken embarrassment. Not tonight. Every time Kyle delved inside me, my back arched, my head thrown back as I got a view of the sky. I couldn't decipher if the stars I saw belonged to the night's sky or the heady feeling his tongue caused me. My previous drinks rushed through my body and mixed with the euphoria of his lips as he sucked on my clit. I wrapped my legs around his face and over his shoulders, pulling his head deeper against me. My hands shook as he ate me out, and I was afraid I'd slip off the tub ledge. I never wanted him to stop.

"Oh, God, oh, Kyle. I'm going to come."

My eyes hooded over. He kept his pressure constant, sucking on my clit, then taking lap after lap while cradling my ass. My pussy clenched, and I began to moan. My hips bucked and I came, my body shuddering, the pleasure rippling throughout every part of me.

"You good, baby?" I liked the way those words sounded.

I whimpered out a yes as I sat up. I motioned for him to stand, and he smirked.

He stood close to me in the corner of the hot tub, and I was mesmerized by his body. He said he played football, and it showed. He was in amazing shape. In better shape than the other pro athletes I'd seen out on the field. He almost looked like one of those fitness models that graced the covers of my workout magazines.

I lifted, swiveled my legs around, and hopped off the ledge, snatching my discarded clothes. Placing them as a makeshift cushion for my knees, I lifted myself back in place and knelt on the ledge of the spa, my naked ass up in the air for anyone to see. I wasn't an exhibitionist but this view made me carefree, it was so hot.

I wrapped my hands around his waist and pulled his trunks down, releasing his cock. My eyes widened. Holy shit, he was huge. I was thrilled and a tad scared. I'd never been with a man this big. But I couldn't wait to be fucked by him.

Clasping my hand around the base of his cock, my mouth opened for him. The hand failed to completely wrap around his thick girth, and my mouth watered.

"Suck me, baby."

I obeyed, licking my lips and doing my best to take him deeply, my lips stretching out, his length tickling the back of my throat. He reached down and guided the back of my neck as my head bobbed. Saliva ran down his length and onto my swollen lips and chin as I took him in and out. I never wanted to stop. He groaned once, then twice before pulling my hair, making me look at him. His eyes hooded, and though I could've sucked him all night, he pulled back. I moaned in protest.

"You want me?" His voice had a powerful rumble, and the authority he held over my movements caused me to grow wetter. He motioned toward the bedroom. His eyes narrowed on a condom on the table next to the bed. Funny, I hadn't noticed that there when I entered the room earlier. He must have taken it out when he changed.

"Yes. Please don't make me wait."

His lips turned into a smile, and he lifted me as if I weighed nothing, threw me over his shoulder, and carried me inside the room. He placed me on the bed on all fours, smacking my ass. "Don't move." My back curled like a cat when I heard the condom foil ripping and glanced back to see him rolling the condom over his thick cock. And though the swim trunks had looked amazing on him, his naked body was even better. He finished covering his cock and gave it a few hard strokes as he stared at my ass. Oh, God, I was so fucking wet, so slick, so ready for him.

He moved with purpose as he rounded the bed, lifting one muscular, long leg and letting it sink into the mattress, gathered my hair at the nape and tugged. I moaned when his lips crashed onto mine, kissing me. Perfectly measured. Not too slow. Yet not fast. Firm. Amazing. More sensually than I thought humanly possible, he swirled his expert tongue with mine. I was gravitating into ecstasy. With one last kiss, he released me and climbed fully on the bed, urging me forward toward the headboard. I crawled forward, stopping at his monster-sized pillows. And he followed. Reaching around me, he stacked the fluffy pillows, placing them in front of me. "Knees on the pillows, beautiful." Immediately, I did as I was told. And he slapped my ass, gripped my left hip, and slid the other arm around me, his hand splayed on my stomach. Pulling my back to his front, he positioned me tightly against him. The firm hand left my middle and I felt it squeeze my right breast.

"Kyle..." Breath panting, I laid my head back on his chest as he groped the breast, rubbing the entire hand back and forth on the nipple.

I writhed against him, purposely sticking my ass out, and let his dick cradle between my ass cheeks. "Fuck me. Please."

This made him chuckle. Teasing me, he let go of my breast and grabbed his dick, before smacking each cheek again. "Ass all the way up, doll. I want you to guide my dick inside you." I lifted higher as he gripped both hips, and pressed his cock inside.

"Ah." I whimpered and he thrust into me. Hard. He felt incredible, pumping deeper, faster. My pussy clenched.

Almost out of breath, I reached forward, gripping the headboard, as he relentlessly pounded in me. And I couldn't get enough. He released my hips and kneaded my ass with one hand and with his other hand worked my clit, rubbing me the right way.

I came like I'd never come before, screaming his name. He kept at it, never losing his pace, and I came again, thrashing over his cock. My entire body hummed from head to toe when he didn't stop, strumming my clit till I came again. Once, twice, three times a lady. I lay limp as his body tense and he released.

He fucked me senseless three more times before morning. In between sessions we talked about our careers and what we planned to do with our lives next. I'd brought it up, wanting to know more. When he mentioned his football career, he told me he was almost sure he was giving it up. That I could consider him a former player. When he'd said it, it was as if a huge weight had been lifted off his shoulders. I was too worried about telling him I had recently made the squad, since he spoke of leaving the sport. It was small talk after that. And a lot of kissing before he wore me out in every room in his house. The next morning, I met his personal trainer, Pat, over breakfast. And after he had left, Kyle and I went at it again, this time in the shower. I'd never come so many times in a twenty-four-hour period. It almost seemed too good to be true. Body sore and sated, I gave him my number and he promised to call. I always believed things which started fast ended fast. All I knew was I didn't want this night to be just another tally for his playbook.

3

KYLE

EARLY DECEMBER, CAMP RHINO, AFGHANISTAN

When I was in college, winter had always been my favorite time of the year. Spring breaks always sucked because I'd been deep into a grueling spring training schedule, while summer vacations I'd spent preparing for the upcoming season. But winter breaks were the one time each year I could escape, party, and hook up without a care in the world.

Not anymore. Most of the time I could barely tell what season it was. In Afghanistan, the long, frigid days and nights blended together. Nowadays, I was checking out terrorists instead of sexy coeds. And strangely enough, I was fulfilled.

Today, I'd get a reprieve from my smelly men. Our SEAL team was the first stop on the much appreciated Christmas USO tour. Kept the morale high. The first plane had arrived yesterday, and the second one had just landed now.

Pat, Vic, and I were on our way to greet the planes. No idea who was on the tour—usually it was a mix of professional athletes, cheerleaders, comedians, and movie stars. I'd done a USO tour myself when I'd played professional ball. Hanging out with the SEALs during Christmastime was what had convinced me to leave my career behind and join the Teams.

My father was a retired Marine, and I'd always wanted to serve my country. It was the best decision I'd ever made.

I handed Vic the big "Welcome to Afghanistan" sign, and the three of us walked to the runway to welcome the USO company. Yup, I was right—a few huge guys walked down the jet way. I immediately recognized one of them, a top quarterback. I was about to shake his hand when Pat whispered in my ear, "Hey, bro, isn't that Omelet Girl?"

I looked up. Fuck my life. Sara, the girl I'd met in Pacific Beach one night last summer while hanging out with Vic walked down the jet way in a skintight sweat suit emblazoned with a flame on the jacket. Pat had nicknamed her Omelet Girl because he'd stopped by my place the morning after I'd met her, and she'd cooked us omelets. They were damn good omelets, too. Vic had bitched those eggs should have technically been his since he'd been my wingman the night before. That only caused Pat to fuck with him some more. But besides being a good cook, I knew next to nothing about the girl. She'd never told me she was a professional cheerleader. A fucking San Diego Wildfire Girl—part of the hottest dance team in the league. Then again, I'd never told her I was a Navy SEAL. I guess we were even.

My eyes traced her body, her incredible curves hiding beneath her clothes. I flashed and remembered her legs spread on the rim of my hot tub as I ate her for all I was worth.

"Hi, Sara." I grinned. "Welcome to Afghanistan, beautiful."

Her mouth flew open and closed, her lips twisting as if temporarily lost in thought. And I wondered if she'd call me out on what I'd done. After a beat, she gave me the same unabashed grin I'd given her. Though hers was more of a smirk. "Kyle! What are you doing here? Wait, you're on the USO tour, too?" she asked excitedly, fluttering her lashes in a dramatic fashion. It was clear she was giving me a hard time. I excepted as much.

She stared at my uniform, realization settling across her face. "Why are you in cammies? Were you on the other plane? Are you playing again? Which team do you play for?"

Whoa, she should've been an interrogator. She could probably do a better job than I could. I laughed and pulled her to my side as she noticeably cringed at the barrage of questions. "SEAL Team Seven, sweetheart—I don't play ball anymore. You just flew thirty-six hours to entertain me. And I'm ready. Come here, baby. Give me a kiss." I hugged her and kissed her cheek, pressing her tight little body up against me.

But our moment ended abruptly when she pulled away from me, her eyes sending me a pained look. Guilt crashed over me—we'd spent an incredible night together, then I'd deployed without saying good-bye. I'd told her I'd call her but never had.

An older lady with bleached-blonde hair and a Botoxed face who resembled an alien nudged Sara, uttering, "I'm going to get set up in the USO barracks. Don't take long. We'll reconvene in the morning." Sara nodded. Probably the chaperone. Those cheerleaders usually traveled with their directors; like modern-day chastity belts. She gave Sara a look that screamed, "Keep it moving!" before walking away. Fuck that, to get some alone time with her I'd throw a flash bang grenade if I had to. Despite her wholesome all-American good girl cheerleader image, Sara was a freak—our night together was one for the books. And I needed a replay.

Her body flinched at the sound of a mortar going off in the distance, and I held her close, cradling her through the blast. The pink sky hung above us, thick with smoke.

"I can't believe you're here. I couldn't figure out why you'd vanished. I thought we'd connected." She paused and her eyes focused on my gun. "A Navy SEAL? That's why you gave up football?"

"Absolutely. I love football but now my life has a different meaning. But football will always be a huge part of my life. I loved playing. Out here, football is important to the men and women who serve. That's how we tell time. Each game means the passing of another week. Another week closer to going home." Vic and Pat stepped over to us. "You remember Vic and Pat, don't you?"

Her girlfriends now gathered to her side and I recognized Sara's friend, Maya, from the club. They were extremely close. There were seven other cheerleaders: a redhead, two brunettes, another blonde, a Latina girl, an Asian girl, and a sister. It was like an ice cream shop of hot women—one flavor for any taste.

"Yeah. Hey, Vic," she greeted, blushing. Vic tipped his head in return. "And Pat was your 'trainer,' right?"

Pat smirked and gave her a reverent hug. Most SEALs lied about their jobs. Trainer was the job I'd given him when he'd met Sara. His eyes made a respectful dance around her friends, but he maintained his distance. Ever since he'd married Annie, Pat kept himself in check. He didn't want any temptation. His only goal these days was to stay alive so he could return home to her and their son in one piece, especially now that Annie was pregnant again.

The rest of the plane had disembarked now. There were other military men attending to the sports players' accommodations. My men had gladly volunteered to take care of the cheerleaders. Well, mostly Vic and I. I grabbed Sara's luggage and escorted her and her fellow cheerleaders to the barracks with the guys trailing behind me. One look from me told them they needed to help the other ladies out. I would be the one assisting Sara. Hopefully in more ways than one. They were to stay in the Distinguished Visitor quarters—small single rooms each, with their own bed and dresser. Much better than the shithole barracks I bunked in. With any luck, I'd be crashing with her tonight.

As the guys made their way down the hall with the other girls, I placed her suitcase in her room, dust flying everywhere.

"So you're a cheerleader? Girl, I knew you were a dancer," I lightly teased, causing her to smile.

She sat on the edge of the bed. The chin-length bob she'd rocked in the nightclub had magically grown into waist-length curls. My mom was a hairdresser; I knew extensions when I saw them. "I'm in college getting a degree in education. Why didn't you tell me you were a SEAL? I think it's awesome." She wasn't letting me off the hook that easily.

Her legs were crossed, indicating she was somewhat closed off to me, but I could only concentrate on the outline of her panties through her sweats. That side view was what dreams were made of. I loved my job, but I missed being around women. Their voices, sweet-smelling hair, and soft bodies were intoxicating.

I simply wasn't used to giving accountability to anyone but my Team. And of course, my mother. But even she didn't know about my missions. "Don't take it personally. I don't tell anyone what I do. It's safer that way. If a guy goes around boasting he's a SEAL, he's probably a liar."

"That makes sense..." her voice trailed off. She avoided making eye contact with me. Yup, I'd hurt her by not calling. Time for damage control.

I knelt by the side of her bed and clutched her hands in mine. It was easier to be accepted at eye level than standing with our vast height difference. "I want to apologize for never telling you I was about to deploy. That's why I didn't call you. I thought we bonded, for real, but since I was leaving I didn't see the point of starting anything. That would have made it harder on you in the long run."

She nodded and bit her bottom lip. "It's cool. I get it. I do." She didn't. Not even a little. But I kept my mouth shut. "I figured you'd thought I was a slut for going home with you the night we met. I don't normally do that, I swear."

All girls wanted you to believe you were the only man

they'd hop into bed with. I didn't doubt her, but I wasn't one of those men who actually cared if she was easy since I was a player. I loved a woman who knew what she wanted—in and out of the bedroom. I didn't want no damn virgin. "I believe you. But you're here now. You're like an angel sent to me. Call or no call, I missed you," I relented. "I'll take care of you while you're here and make sure you're safe." It was a genuine offer. Some of the shit I had seen left me with nightmares. But I was damn good at my job.

I touched her shoulder and watched her body shiver. I wasn't going to push myself on her, but I hadn't gotten laid since that night. I'd be damned if I wasn't going to try. Besides, I really liked her. With just one night, she'd kept me on my toes.

Her body responded to me, her chest heaved, her mouth moistened. That was all I needed to see. I kissed her, my beard scratching her soft skin.

"Kyle, I've thought about our night together so many times. But I don't want to get kicked off the team. We have strict rules about not entertaining the men."

I placed my finger over her lips. "It's okay, baby. If you want to spend some alone time with me while you're here, I can arrange that. I want you. But the ball's in your court. Trust me. No one's going to know."

Her eyes widened but her brows furrowed. After an awkward pause, she finally spoke, her voice cracking. "Yeah. Sure. Why not? I'm game." Her eyes told me she didn't agree with what she'd said. But I wasn't about to question her. She rubbed her fingers over my chest and traced them down to just above my cock. I groaned inwardly, my balls tightening. Yep. I was in for a world of hurt tonight. My length grew inside my cammies, and I wanted to take her then and there, but I needed to wait.

She fought a yawn, but it overtook her. I knew she must've been tired, after her long travel day. I had a week to be around her, take care of her every need, and maybe she'd take care of mine. Plus, I couldn't wait to see her dance in those tight, white boy shorts the girls on her cheer team wore.

"You've got a big day tomorrow. I'll work something out for after the show."

"I'm glad you're here, Kyle." Her plump, pink lips parted, begging me to kiss them.

"Get a good night's rest. I'm your personal security guard for the week. I'll see you tomorrow." I kissed her with gusto, showing just how much I wanted her, and cupped her ass in my free hand. Then left before I got both of us in trouble. I walked back to my barracks, adjusting myself as I went. I'd plan a date with her tomorrow night. Shit, Pat owed me one. He'd find a way to hook a brother up.

I didn't normally believe in fate—Pat and Annie were always talking about how they were destined to meet and be together. But that was for suckers, right? Shit. I shook my head. Could it be true? What were the chances of Sara and me meeting in San Diego, both omitting parts of our lives, and reuniting all the way across the world? I wasn't gonna lie. The cheerleader and football player had a nice ring to it.

4

SARA

I savored Kyle's taste on my lips, desperate for another kiss. He was so fine, looked even hotter than when I'd seen him last. His sleeves rolled up on his cammies revealed his incredible bicep, his pants clung to his strong thighs. He'd sported a full beard that had been absent in the club, making him look even more masculine. Dangerous. Badass.

I was still baffled. What were the odds of him being here? We'd spent one amazing night together. Afterward, he'd asked for my number, but never called. That had stung. Badly. I'd assumed besides unfairly judging me for what we both willingly participated in, maybe he was just such a player and he never intended it to be anything more than a one-night stand.

The name tape on his uniform read: Lawson. Kyle Lawson. Not proud of it, but I had cyber stalked him after our time together. He'd told me he was a football player, and his face did look vaguely familiar. So I had Googled every Kyle who'd ever played professional football, but had come up empty-handed. I knew for sure he didn't play for San Diego. But now I remembered reading a story a few years back about a football player who had turned down a multi-million dollar contract to join the military. I swore that guy had a different name. Terrence? Trevor? Was that Kyle? Sure sounded like him. Maybe SEALs used fake names? I wanted to look it up now. It wasn't stalking. It was research. Dammit—the lack of Internet over here in these barracks really killed me. I was suffering serious withdrawal. People nowadays were completely too dependent on electronics, especially smart phones, and I was no exception. I clutched my useless iPhone, which at the moment only acted as a photo album. Our director had mentioned how long these guys' tours were. I couldn't imagine living here for seven months—how did these men do it? They had my upmost respect. Finding out the lack of communication these men had made me feel a bit better about never hearing from Kyle. I still couldn't believe I'd bumped into him, here of all places.

A strong rap at the door startled me. Had he come back so soon? I opened the door, but instead of Kyle standing there, I was greeted with the scowl from my director.

"Hi Denise. I was just about to crash. Do we need to do anything?"

Her eyes leveled me. "No, just a night check to make sure that you're alone. I saw that SEAL seemed to be awfully friendly with you."

Damn. Nothing got past her. "Oh, it's nothing like that. I know him."

Her lips pursed. "That's what I was afraid of. Look, Sara, you're a rookie. Four hundred girls tried out to be on this team and I chose you. Don't make me regret my decision. The Wildfire organization has strict rules regarding fraternizing with the military men while we are on tour. If you embarrass me, I'll kick you off the squad. Are we clear?"

She was a buzz killer. "Absolutely. You don't have to worry. I'm on my best behavior."

She gave me a condescending nod—as if she read my dirty

thoughts about Kyle. "Good night, Sara." She left the room and slammed the door.

I nervously pulled my hair. It was too risky to hook up with Kyle while I was here. I didn't want to get kicked off the squad when I'd worked so hard to get here.

But maybe, I could get away with it. Kyle was a SEAL. If anyone could smuggle me out of this room, he could. Their motto was, "We are U.S. Navy SEALs. There's no need to thank us because we don't exist. You never saw us. This never happened." Yeah, if he could extract a hostage, he could definitely pluck a sex-starved cheerleader from a barracks room.

A Navy SEAL. I was almost certain he was the man I'd read about. How many men would give up millions of dollars to join the military? My mind was blown. Was his love for his country so deep? I couldn't fathom giving up my lifestyle to fight a war. But I guess that's what it meant to be a SEAL.

My brothers hated SEALs. Die-hard jarheads, my siblings loved God, family, and the Marine Corps. They were always saying how they thought SEALs were a bunch of cocky assholes. And I was supposed to agree. The thing was, I didn't. At least I didn't think I did. I knew a great guy whom just so happened to be a SEAL.

Besides, my brothers loved football. Kyle definitely loved it as well. They'd probably get along great. And then it hit me. I was defending him as if what we had was real.

Stop thinking that, Sara. He was a hookup—not a boyfriend. Your family will never meet him. He didn't even call you.

Still it was hard to be fully upset with him. I knew Kyle was a special man when I'd met him. But I had no idea how amazing he was. This one act of leaving football, something he clearly loved so much, to serve our country showed me there was more to Kyle than just physical strength. Yes, he was a sex god with rock-hard abs and a glinting smile. But more importantly, he was selfless. He fascinated me. He was someone who I wanted to get to know, who I needed to learn what made him tick.

He was someone I could fall in love with.

Sara, stop!

I closed my eyes and forced my mind to calm and return to reality. I could never fall in love with this man and he most definitely wouldn't fall in love with me. I didn't always have the smoothest history with men. Except for my brothers, the men I had gotten attached to tended to leave me high and dry, starting with my father. Soon, after weeks went by without a call, I knew I'd almost made the same mistake again. Sure, tonight Kyle had been excited to see me, but that was because I was probably his only hope of getting laid for the remainder of this deployment. I was a sure thing. My oldest brother once told me the second a man met a woman the man decided in that moment if she was going to be a hookup or a girlfriend. I wasn't naïve enough to believe I was the latter. Kyle saw me as a fling. And that's all I'd be to him. It wasn't rocket science.

And honestly, it was better this way. Clear expectations from both sides, with no hope for a future. It was what it was. Kyle wanted hot sex with no ties or drama, and honestly so did I. He would never make me false declarations of love. There was no expectation of him ever staying with me.

And my heart wouldn't be crushed when he left. So why did it feel like I was giving up my needs just like he'd given up his football career?

5

KYLE

I awoke the next day at zero six hundred, and for a second I thought seeing Sara had been a dream. Once I came to, I hurriedly got dressed. Pat and Vic were already waiting for me. The rest of the guys on my Team were beginning their day as well.

Pat slapped me on the back. "So, you want me to distract, maybe kick up a sandstorm, so you can get some alone time together?" My boys always had my six.

"Sounds like a plan. How's Annie?" Communication here was limited, so Pat had to deal with hearing news late sometimes. There were so many dudes here that all of them wanted a piece of the action. Thank goodness for the communication hall, even if our allowed time did suck ass.

"Good. No longer having morning sickness. At least that's what she told me last time we were able to talk. We find out the baby's gender on Friday. I'm excited to find out, man. But I'm sure it's a boy."

Vic cackled. "In your dreams, Walsh. It's a girl, and you know it."

Had to hand it to Vic—he was probably right. All Team

guys ended up with girls. Frogman's curse. Something about our balls being frozen in the cold water made our sperm only shoot out X's. One of our buddies had six daughters. Six! That was a Team in itself. But I'd show these fools how it was done. When I decided to have children, I'd take a month of leave and head to Hawaii first. Warm that shit up.

I glanced at the schedule: Two meet and greets with the football players, performance from the cheerleaders, and autographs. There were hundreds of soldiers here, so the shows would be split in two. I'd be attending the first show. Then tomorrow they'd be transferred to the next base and repeat the same routine. They'd only return here on select nights till they left.

We skipped the football player meet and greet—been there, done that. But no way in hell was I going to miss Sara dancing for me.

I dragged Vic and Kyle early to the auditorium. American flags adorned the concrete walls, and plastic fold-up chairs filled the floor. I needed a good seat. Within minutes, the hall was filled with sailors, SEALs, and Marines.

After a cheesy introduction by some nameless comedian, the girls took the stage. I only had eyes for one. Sweet Jesus, Sara was fine. She came out in cutoff daisy dukes, a red tank top, and blue cowboy boots. It wasn't the typical white shorts the dancers normally wore but I'd take it. She discreetly blew a kiss in my direction. Any guy who may have seen it probably sported an instant hard-on. Yeah. She had that much pull.

The lights dimmed, and the unmistakable guitar riffs of AC/DC's classic "You Shook Me All Night Long" began. Her eyes glued on me, Sara twirled her hips, whipping her hair back and forth. It was as if she was my own personal dancer. And every time her eyes glossed over with need, I pictured her face when I'd made her come. She'd sported the same intoxicating expression. Her movements were perfectly in sync with her squad, but Sara stood out. The curves of her body, the precision of her steps, the warmth radiating from her smile. I'd seen tons of dancers in my time, on and off the pole, but Sara was in a class of her own. The audience was mesmerized. I closed my eyes for a second, imagining we were back in the club in San Diego, and she was dancing only for me—not for a room full of horny men.

The song ended, and the roars from the claps echoed throughout the room. Maya grabbed the microphone. "Hi, everyone. As captain of the Sparks, on behalf of the San Diego Wildfires and ourselves, I want to thank you for inviting us here to perform for you all. It's truly an honor for everyone on the squad to be entertaining our heroes."

The audience clapped as Sara took the microphone next. And the guys grew louder when she winked. "Hello, everyone. I'm Sara. For this next number, we're looking for three volunteers." Her gaze turned to me, and my hand popped up in the air, like some involuntary response.

Of course, she chose me. By the way she was just eye-fucking the shit out of me, it wasn't even a question. And then two other men were chosen, a Marine and sailor. She ran off the stage, emerging a minute later dressed as a sexy Santa.

Another cheerleader pulled out three chairs and motioned toward me and the two other men to sit. Score, I'd be getting some sort of a private dance after all. Just a very public one. One where I couldn't touch her like I wanted.

Each guy had a cheerleader by their side. Then the song "Santa Baby" started playing. Modernly sang, it was the Taylor Swift version, and not my favorite rendition by Eartha Kitt. I had more memories associated with the original. But since Sara danced around me, waving some feathery boa in my face, I didn't give a fuck who sang. As long as I had a good view of her ass, Humpty Dumpty could be playing. I'd get down with nursery rhymes. Fuck it.

I relaxed into the chair, thoroughly enjoying my PG lap dance. Pat and Vic were laughing their asses off at me. Fuck them, this dance was the closest any of us got to getting laid since we'd arrived. Those two could go jerk off in their racks later tonight, alone. I was going to get some pussy.

The song ended too soon and Sara kissed me on the cheek. So did the other two shitheads picked. I'd take what I could get for now but would arrange something for later tonight.

When I thought no one was looking, I whispered in her ear, "Leave your window open."

Momentarily, she froze. Her upper lip quivered, but she was a good actress. She gave me a friendly hug, and shooed me off the stage.

Back in the audience with Pat and Vic, I formulated a plan. All I needed was the top of an empty bunker, a sleeping bag, and her willing body. It was going to be a banging night. In more ways than one.

6

SARA

Finally, a computer. With Internet.

Following our hour-long show, I was exhausted. Afterward, we did autographs and were shown around the place a bit. We practiced for our next show and now, here I was. I really wanted to soak in a bathtub, maybe with some Epsom Salt. But warm baths were one of the many luxuries that would have to wait till I returned home.

I had a small break before dinner and then another meet and greet. All my girls were checking their emails or Facebook on the computers in the communication hall. I however, had more important things to research. I picked a spot in the back and got to work.

"Kyle Lawson football."

Articles popped up. *Terrell* Kyle Lawson. So Kyle was his middle name—seemed like a clandestine SEAL maneuver. I clicked on the Wiki link.

Terrell Kyle Lawson is an American football player who left his professional career and became an officer in the United States Navy. He turned down a five-year, 9.6 million dollar contract with the Oakland Marauders. Popularly known by his initials, T.K., Lawson is as renowned for his refusal to grant any media interviews as he is for his talent on the field.

He gave up 9.6 million dollars?! I knew he was special. To some, that action would seem like he ripped up a winning lottery ticket.

Article after article rehashed the same story with no new insight, mainly because Kyle had refused all media interviews. Which made perfect sense because anonymity was important to be a member of the SEALs. Despite all the recent SEAL memoirs, SEALs were supposed to be silent operators. That much even I knew.

Maya pulled her chair next to mine. "I can't believe he's the same guy we met at Green Flash Bar & Grill. That's crazy. His boy Vic is fine as hell with his insane body and never-ending tats—thank God I didn't hook up with him though. I remember that night I just thought both of them were players. I would never date a SEAL. And neither should you."

I rolled my eyes at her. "It's totally fate—we were meant to see each other again. I honestly believe that. Yes, he may be cocky. But there's more to him than that." I pointed to the screen. "Case in point. Check this out. Did you know he turned down a 9.6-million dollar contract to become a SEAL?"

She studied the computer screen, and crinkled her face. "That's pretty stupid if you ask me. I mean, think of all the good he could do with that money. There's no law that says you have to blow it on mansions, a Maserati, or frivolous bullshit, Sara. He could've saved a ton of homeless dogs or donated to a women's shelter." I knew she was right, but his decision did not lose its luster in my eyes. It was still humble.

"All good points. But he told me at his place that he wanted to live his life with a purpose. And this is the path he chose. I have to respect it. Plus, it's totally hot."

She twirled her hair, giving me a vacant stare. "First off, that's a line. One that you fell for. You're always trying to give people the benefit of the doubt. And secondly, even if he meant it, it's stupid, not hot. Do you know how dangerous his job is? Sounds like he's chasing a high. He's an adrenaline junky. Seriously, Sara, you know these SEALs. All the ones I've met are cheaters. One girl on our squad dated one and he cheated on her with a stripper. A stripper! You need to stay far away from him. Did you forget he fucked you seven ways to Sunday and never called you? You know that every chick in San Diego drops their panties at the first sign of a SEAL. You don't need to deal with that shit. You're beautiful, smart, love kids, are a professional cheerleader, and have a career ahead of you as a teacher. I mean you work part time at a preschool. I thought you wanted to get married in a couple of years and have a family? Kyle's not the type to settle down. You can get any guy you want. Don't waste your time on a player." Jesus. She needed to take a breath. She sounded so judgmental right now. Just knowing the girls she knew boasted about being with SEALs told me those girls were with attention seekers too. Most SEALs never spoke about their careers. Did she ever think of that? Okay, so he wasn't perfect. Who was? Definitely not me. Then again, I'd known Maya for way too long. The rant she just unloaded on me came from a good place. And she wasn't wrong about the things I wanted.

I nodded my head in agreement, forcing my heart to listen, but it refused. Fine, he was a player, but every player can be tamed for the right woman, right? And I didn't blame him for not calling me, after all—we hadn't exactly started our relationship out on the right foot. I was equally at fault. It was exhausting going back and forth on what he represented to me and what I wanted out of us hooking up. Emotional whiplash was a real bitch.

Maya clutched my arm. "Aye, Sara, seriously. No. Forget about him. I don't care that he fucked you like a porn star. He'll never be faithful to you. A SEAL and a baller? It's the worst combination. He probably gets more pussy than an animal shelter."

"Nice, Maya," I groaned.

She kept going. "Not to mention you're on a USO tour. If you sneak away to hook up with him, you'll get kicked off the squad. Did I ever tell you about Emma? She was on the squad a few years ago. Well she was caught blowing the bassist for Möxie Cörps. They flew her ass home, made her turn in her poms, and even the website erased any trace of her. You can't get anything past Denise. She's like a hawk. Take it from your captain. If she finds out, you're as good as gone. All you ever wanted was to be a cheerleader, and you worked so hard. Don't throw it away on this guy's jock." Damn it.

"You're right."

Maya pursed her lips, and shook her head. She knew me well enough to know I was already fixated on Kyle. But she didn't need to sound so matter of fact about it. What the hell? Was I destined to be alone? What was wrong with having a good time? I could handle this. I turned back to the computer. At least she stopped the nagging, stood up, and left.

I closed out the articles on Kyle and logged into my Facebook, reading my messages. My mom worried about me being overseas, and my friends back home wanted to know if I'd met any sexy male celebrities on the tour. Yes, there were some hot movie stars on the USO tour, but none of them were worth mentioning at all. I only had eyes for Kyle.

7

KYLE

As an officer of SEAL Team Seven, I planned our missions. The logistics, the equipment, the operations, every detail. I didn't take a vote, I made the final decisions. Tonight, I was planning an important operation—Operation Rapunzel.

With her now long blonde hair, the name fit her to a T. After handing out assignments, I ditched Pat and Vic, and went to Sara's room. My guys were trained well enough; little instructions were needed. I needed to see her before she left on the convoy. With any luck, she'd be waiting for me.

Luckily, she followed my instructions; her window was open. And it was dark. This was too easy. I climbed into the opening, careful not to wake her fellow cheerleaders or the virgin patrol mistress in the adjacent rooms.

Sara was curled up on her bed, her hair wild, her eyelids closed. The day's events had definitely taken a toll on her. She wore a pink tank top with no bra and white pajama bottoms. I stared at her from the window. Her nipples were erect, and I wanted to suck them until she screamed my name.

I continued to stare around the room and at the walls:

barren, white, thin. Nothing could happen in here. I didn't want to waste any time. In two quick strides, I was at the bed. I bent and kissed her, gently rousing her from her sleep.

She rubbed her eyes and stretched her back. And I placed my finger over her lips, urging her to stay quiet.

Before she knew what was happening, I scooped her into my arms and smuggled her out of her room. She was so light; my seabag was heavier than her.

I snuck her behind the barracks, across our communications building, to a row of empty bunkers. She kept silent, and clung to my chest, waiting to see what I'd do next.

I placed a finger to my lips again and motioned for her to climb up the stairs to the top of the bunker. Her eyes grew to the size of saucers, and I chuckled softly. "I've got you." It was quite comical that at six-feet-five and two-hundred fifty pounds she thought I would possibly let her fall. Still, she hesitated at first, but began her ascent, as I followed closely under her, my face just inches from her round ass.

Once up top, I pulled a thick sleeping bag out of my backpack, threw it down, and pulled Sara close to me. "I'm a regular Boy Scout," I laughed, and she grinned, showing me a shy smile.

"Wow, how'd you know about this spot? Better yet, how many ladies have you brought up here?"

"Just you, sweetheart. But this is known internally as the hookup bunker. It's far enough away from the barracks and watch spots to be inconspicuous. Occasionally I come up here to relax or pray, but I do that alone. It's hard to find any peace here."

Her head tilted in a thoughtful way. "Pray? Are you religious?"

"Yes, ma'am. Son of a preacher man. After my dad left the Corps, he became a man of God. What about you?" It was nice finding out more about her.

"I'm Southern Baptist. But I haven't gone to church since I was in high school," she admitted, her eyes downcast.

I moved a lock of hair out of her face, bringing her head back up so she could meet my eyes. "It's okay that you haven't gone in a while. Personally, I lost my way when I was playing ball." My cheeks burned, a physical reminder of my shame. It was harder to take your own advice than to dish it out. "The women, the money, the drugs, shit, the lifestyle. I'm no saint, but seeing so much life and death really makes you want to believe in something bigger than yourself."

Her lips widened into a smile, and she snuggled on my chest. She fit perfectly. There was an ease in talking to her that I hadn't had with another woman in years. It felt like I'd known her forever. She didn't make me feel like half the prick I really was. As if she saw the good in me even if sometimes I couldn't see it myself.

Leaning in, I gave her a chaste kiss. There was no urgency behind it; I just wanted to be close to her, share the moment with her by my side. It was one hell of a scene. I took in the moonlit sky. Its many stars. The rarely quiet Afghani mountains. No commotions. Just quiet. Just us.

"So, what's your deal? Why don't you have a man?"

I was only teasing her, but she looked away from me. She did that often. As if she doubted herself a lot. Or somewhere down the line, she was told she was a disappointment and she believed it. Didn't know why. I thought she was pretty damned cool. Whomever made her feel that way was a fucking imbecile. It was sobering to see we all had our hang-ups. We carried that extra weight on our backs as validation, trudging through life without justification, just feeding off of the bullshit we were fed.

"Oh, I don't know," she began, "it's nothing dramatic. I've been so focused on practicing once I made the squad that I didn't have time to date. I go to school full time, so a lot of my time is spent studying. Work mornings at a preschool, I dance, and work out the rest of the time." She continued to talk but stayed looking away. "I had a boyfriend my first two years in college, but he was a bit controlling, didn't want me to try out. I guess he was afraid I'd leave him or get hit on. He left me when I made the squad. So after we broke up, I didn't want to date another guy who would be against my dreams."

"Sara?"

"Yeah?"

"Look at me, sweetheart. I'd like to see your face while we're talking." She tilted her face in my direction. "Much better."

She let out a calmed breath, and wet her lips. "What about you? A Navy SEAL and a former football player? You must have women throwing themselves at you."

I laughed. There was my girl. "I'm not gonna lie, I've had my share. But once they found out I played ball, they only saw dollar signs." Her nose scrunched at the comment. "I had a girlfriend for a bit when I was playing, but once I told her I wanted to leave football and join the Teams, she bailed. So I'll be real with you, Sara. You're gorgeous, a sweetheart, smart, and I'm glad you're here, but I'm not looking for anything serious. It's nothing personal. This job just has a way of destroying relationships. It wouldn't be fair to get involved with you when I'm deployed nine months out of the year. I don't want to lead you on."

She swallowed and pursed her lips in thought. I felt bad but I prided myself on being honest about my intentions, about every aspect of my life. And I believed what I was saying. I was married to the Teams. I pledged my life to this job. A hookup with a beautiful woman was my reward for all the ways my career took over every aspect of my personal life. I needed her, I needed this release.

After an uncomfortable pause, she moved in closer and straddled me. "It's okay, neither am I. Fair catch?"

I loved it when a woman talked football to me. "Fair catch."

I pulled her under me, pressing myself between her thighs. She gasped and her mouth broke into a smile. The cool breeze from the mountain air seemed almost haunting, the landscape binding us together. My beard scraped her cheek, and I slowly lowered my lips to hers. She was so fucking beautiful. The first time we'd had sex, it had been all about urgency, lust, a desire for carnal knowledge. This time I wanted to take it slow, explore her, find comfort in her embrace. Kissing her was the only time I'd found peace since I'd arrived in this country and I didn't want our connection to end. I was busy working for the rest of the week so this would be my only chance to steal her away. Come tomorrow, she'd be gone most of the day. And I wasn't certain that I'd be able to get another moment with her.

She welcomed my kiss, her soft lips kissing me back, gently, her hot tongue exploring my mouth. Her hands clutched my ass, her fingers urging me closer to her, erasing the distance between us.

Pulling back, I reached under her tank top, my right hand cupping her left breast. I focused on the pert nipple and gave it a small pinch, then worked on the other. She had amazing tits. A phenomenal rack. And I fought the desire to yank her top off just for the view. I knew I couldn't. I wasn't about to take her clothes off and strip her down naked on top of this bunker, just in case we got caught. Fuck. This was hard. The forbidden element only made our liaison hotter. She arched her back and I rubbed circles around her nipple before giving it a small tug this time. She moaned softly then sucked on my tongue. Damn it. She kept that shit up and I was gonna blow my load before we even got started. "Easy," I warned, taking a deep breath. "Lie back, baby." She did as I asked, staring at me through lustful eyes. I stared back, relishing in the beauty that was her body for mere seconds before hooking my middle finger on the hem of her panties, and pulled it back with force. She whimpered, murmuring things I couldn't quite understand. Using her wetness as lubricant, I slid a finger down her center then added two more, pressing into her warmth. Her lips were smooth; completely waxed. I was dying to lick her, taste her sweetness, but not here, not now.

She lay back on the sleeping bag, and I quickly unwrapped a condom, sliding it onto my length.

"Baby," I whispered as I rubbed her clit hard and then soft, "you ready for me?"

She nodded yes, arched her back high off the floor, and I slid her pajama bottoms off as I positioned myself closer between her legs. One long thrust in and she gasped. Man, she was so hot and wet. I felt her hot center stretching for me, adapting to my size. Her tight pussy clamped around my cock. She took me like a champ, her sweet moans driving me wild. With one hand gripping her around the waist, I pulled her hips into me, my finger strumming her clit with the other.

"Oh, Kyle. You feel so good. Don't stop." She groaned each time I pulled out almost completely then slammed back into her. My own grunts sounded off in time with every little moan she gave. She already looked like she was going to come. *Not yet, baby.*

I flipped her over and propped her up so she was on all fours. She looked over her shoulder, her eyes heated, and gave me a playful glance. And I pumped my cock deep inside her, my hand prying her legs farther apart so I was still focused on her clit with two soaked fingers. The squishy sounds of our bodies rubbing together only made me want to pound into her more until she came moaning my name. Our rhythm picked up speed, and just as she would beg me not to stop, I slowed my pace.

"Doll, I could do this all night. I'm not gonna stop until you come all over me. But I want to prolong it for just a little while longer. Don't come yet."

She mewed in response. Her ass shined in the moonlight. My hand came down across her right cheek. Not hard, but firm enough. She had a serious booty. Round, plump, tanned.

I worked her back into me. I could tell she was closer, her breath hitched, her pussy clenched, her body shook. "Ah Kyle. Make me come."

I wasn't done with her yet. I wanted to stare into her eyes, see her body convulse, the look of pleasure flush on her face. I wanted to see the look she gave me earlier, now knowing I deserved it, because I'd put it there.

I reached down. Wrapping a long arm around her middle, I twisted her around again so she sat on me, and fastened my hot mouth on her nipple, licking, sucking, my tongue swirling on the tip for all I was worth.

She pressed into me, swiveling her hips, flipping her hair back, and bit her lip.

"That's it baby. Ride me," I encouraged.

With almost a wicked grin, she rubbed deep against me. Her rhythm varied, her legs wrapped around my back. It was as if she was giving me a private dance, the most incredible lap dance I'd ever had. My dick swelled.

"Oh, Kyle, oh, oh, oh, my God."

"That's it baby."

Her pussy tightened around me, her eyelids closed, and she let out a deep moan. I let myself go, cradling her through her orgasm, completely connected to the beautiful woman on my lap.

That's new.

She gave a final whip back on her sweat-sprinkled hair, and out came a sweet giggle. I pulled her into my arms.

It surprised me I didn't want to bail the moment we were done. In fact, I was dreading her leaving. As I held onto her, the rise and fall of her chest told me she was still catching her breath. The ruins of war surrounded us, and I couldn't help but feel our connection was deeper than a casual hookup, that we'd been placed on the same path for a reason.

But it didn't matter.

Sara could be the perfect woman for me, but it wasn't the right time. I had to let her go.

8

SARA

He held me tighter than ever before, and I didn't want him to leave. Kyle had snuck me back into my barracks without rousing a soul, and for that I was grateful. We shared a tender kiss goodbye and he disappeared almost as fast as he'd appeared. After I stared at the window long after he'd left, I slept blissfully, despite a mortar going off in the background in the middle of the night. The next morning, I woke when our director, Denise, rapped at the door. I knew that knock. Could she have banged any harder? Instinctively, I covered my head with the pillow.

Then for a second, my heart stopped—had she known I'd snuck off in the middle of the night? I sat straight up.

"Sara, we leave in ten minutes."

I took a deep breath; I was paranoid. But I'd definitely slept in. Only my head moved as I stared at the window again. I wondered where on the base was he, and what was he doing? I felt like some love struck teenager. But I knew I wasn't in love, not even close. I was curious. Kyle was hot, and I craved him. He was like every sexual fantasy I'd ever had coming true. A SEAL. A football player. With qualities I admired. Too bad he wasn't interested in a relationship. I wasn't either, but for Kyle, I'd consider making an exception.

I hated being so pathetic and emotionally attached. I was such a cliché. He fucked me just like I liked and I was willing to forget what he'd said. Being with him was a damn pipe dream. Here I thought I was this cool chick in control of my sexuality, able to separate my emotions after sex. But since the night I'd met Kyle in PB, I hadn't been able to stop thinking about him. I hadn't even looked at another man. Sighing, I finally stood up and rushed to get ready.

I guess it was a blessing I wouldn't be seeing him much before we left. Today we were set to tour the next base, and though we'd return here tomorrow night, in five days we'd be back in the States.

And Kyle would remain here. For Christmas. Sure, at some point he'd return to San Diego, for however long SEALs remained in town before their next deployment. But Kyle had made it crystal clear he wasn't interested in anything more than a casual "friends with benefits" situation. And I respected him for being honest with me. Most guys would say anything to get laid. Not that Kyle seemed to have any problems in that department.

My door flew open. But it wasn't my director or Kyle. It was Maya, all done up, hair perfectly curled.

"Damn, girl. You look like shit. Put your face on and I'll do your hair."

I hopped out of bed and put on my travel clothes as Maya went to work on my hair. She pulled back a lock of my hair to tease it and gasped.

"Is that a hickey? Oh my god. You didn't! You hooked up with Kyle!"

I cupped my neck. I didn't remember him giving me a hickey. How could I have been so stupid. I grabbed my compact and dug into my makeup case and slabbed some concealer on it.

"Sara Elizabeth Michaels. Tell me now."

"Okay. Yes. I did. Please lower your voice. He snuck me out of the room. It was incredible."

She just shook her head, clearly disgusted with me. "What were you thinking? I don't care what you do back home—hell you could go fuck an entire SEAL Team and I wouldn't give you a hard time. But we are on a tour. Why are you risking your dream on this guy?"

I wasn't going to argue. I dabbed and dabbed makeup on until the hickey was less noticeable. "Don't tell anyone. Please? It won't happen again."

"Damn straight it won't. I'm sticking with you until we go home. Seriously, Sara. He's not worth it."

I rolled my eyes and reminded myself she was just trying to protect me. I agreed with her, anyhow. That was it. Last time. I would not become his fuck buddy.

I counted my blessings. I was on a USO tour, entertaining our troops who risked their lives for our freedom. How many people could say that? I was a member of one of the best dance squads in the league while still keeping a high GPA. And last night I had the most incredible sex of my life with an amazing man, a hero. I was truly fortunate. The pesky other feelings be damned. Kyle made me feel safe, and I knew that as long as he was in my corner, while I was here, he would never let anything happen to me. That was why I cut him a break. He might not be willing to stick around, but for the short time I was near him, I felt wanted. And that was enough.

9

KYLE

I could still taste Sara on my lips when I awoke the next morning. Images of me fucking her from behind were stored in my head for later use. The way I'd impaled her deeply, until she came all over my cock. She was truly breathtakingly beautiful inside and fine as hell outside. She seemed solid. Non crazy. Sweet. Dared I say, loving. But it didn't matter. I wasn't in the market for a girlfriend. Could still dream about her though. Replay our conversations. Memorize every image from last night for when I was alone. And use her calendar photo as my spank shot. Remember the time she had been mine, if only briefly.

I rolled out of my cot, put on my clothes, and prepared to say good-bye to Sara and her squad. If I got stuck on watch duty after today, I might not see her again. That bothered me.

I found Pat waiting outside my room. Damn early riser. Then again, he wasn't the one that slept like a baby because his world was rocked last night. That pleasure went to yours truly. "How was your night, bro?"

"A gentleman never tells," I joked. "Let's just say I'm surprised that bunker is still standing."

His lips twisted. "Fuck you, man. I miss Annie so much. She saw a picture online of the cheerleaders on the tour and now she's stressing that I'm gonna cheat on her. I know she's pregnant and hormonal, but nothing I say seems to reassure her."

I put my hand on his shoulder. "Sorry, man, that's rough. But Annie's a strong woman. And I know you'd never cheat. Tell her I'd put a bullet in your brain first."

"Of course, I wouldn't cheat on her. I love her, but being married while in the Teams sucks. I miss her and Gabriel. I hope our deployment doesn't get extended because I'll miss our baby's birth."

My chest tightened. I felt for the dude. It sucked. But I selfishly felt reassured because his words proved my point that being married or involved while on the Teams was nonstop headaches and heartbreak. Seeing Pat miss Annie confirmed my belief a relationship while I was in the Teams wasn't right for me. The guilt would eat me alive. And then there was the other downer to relationships. Poor Vic's whore of an ex-wife cheated on him during one of our first deployments. Tore that boy up. No, thank you. I was good. When I settled down, I wanted to be around. Have a family, be there for my kids, coach my son's football team, take my daughter to ballet lessons. Pat and Vic barely saw their kids. It sucked big time. I didn't want to live like that. My father was my hero, an excellent role model, a strong man, a great husband, and a loving father. And until I could be that good of a man, I would remain single. The bar was set high, and I wasn't about to half ass it. I never half assed anything.

Vic emerged from outside and the three of us headed over to the motor T area. The other guys on my Team were used to seeing us three together, well, practically all the time. Didn't mean I appreciated the other men any less. We had already been briefed before the convoy was due to leave. Safety, plans for if there were any interruptions, who was in the lead vehicle.

All the normal things that needed to be discussed between the leaders of the convoy and the soldiers. Which was communicated with my SEAL Team as we were the quick reaction force, in case there were any problems. The convoy crew had done their pre-combat checks. Made sure everyone had weapons, enough ammo, and the vehicles were topped off. The civilians had been briefed as well. If anything were to happen, they were to stay in the vehicles until help had arrived.

We stared ahead. There were ten two-ton vehicles in the convoy to transport the USO performers. Eight up-armored Humvees and two troop carriers. Sara would be in the third vehicle.

The girls were lined up two by two next to the first troop carrier like they were going on an ark, with the chaperone in the back. The cheerleaders would be in one of the troop carriers, and the players in the other. Two soldiers-only Humvees led the pack.

We decided to assist the soldiers in helping the girls climb on board. Sara noticed me and pushed to the front of the line past a few girls and pointedly gave me a somber look. Immediately, my chest constricted. There went the guilt I feared. Feelings I didn't know what the fuck to do with hit me like a ton of bricks. My hand lingered on her back for far too long as I helped her into the assigned vehicle. She pressed her body into my chest, the stance a bittersweet memory. Her noticeable breaths coming out choppy, and she imprinted her scent on me. Which only caused my own uneven breaths.

What the hell was going on? I'd see her tomorrow night. Why was it so hard to let her go?

She didn't look back as Vic loaded the last of the girls into the body of the vehicle.

With everyone safely inside, the drivers turned on the ignitions and the vehicles rumbled to life, taking off around the dirt road. Sand flew through the sky, sprinkling on the vehicles as the guys waved them good-bye. My limbs felt heavy, my hands only managing to form clenched fists, almost hanging lifelessly at my sides.

For a moment I had the urge to run after her, my gut uneasy, a haunting fear I would never see her again weighing me down like quicksand.

10

SARA

Our vehicle rumbled down the dirt road for the next hour, every bump and tremor sending sharp pains through my spine. Afghanistan was a mountainous desert. I'd sat quietly throughout the trip, lost in thought. When we'd left the base, at the last moment, I'd sat up, finally staring back at Kyle. He stood still as a statue while his friends waved enthusiastically, the mountains just past the transportation area serving as a serene but lonely backdrop. He was shutting down. Again. A sob had threatened to escape my lips. I sighed and closed my eyes and tried to compartmentalize the situation, starting with reliving every moment I'd spent last night with Kyle. I'd felt safe. Comfortable. Invincible even. But they weren't enough. One thing I fought was wallowing in those memories. The more I thought about his behavior after, the more upset I became.

My lust and admiration for him now had been replaced by anger and disappointment. Too overcome with nervousness, I'd waited for him to speak. Silently begged him to say anything. He said nothing as I left. Just like he'd done before. Fuck him. I'd done nothing wrong. Fool me once, shame on me. I should have learned. Yet the fresh scorch of rejection burned like hell. I couldn't stomach what was happening between us.

The first time around he should've called me, told me he was going away, even if he didn't want to tell me he was a SEAL. And now he probably thought after our second hookup I would be grateful to be his fuck buddy whenever he returned to the States. I dragged in a heavy breath. How was it he made me feel so amazing one minute and like utter shit the next?

Fuck that, Maya was right. I didn't care how amazing Kyle was, or that he was a humble man dedicated to his country. To him, I was disposable. And I deserved more. I didn't want to be his jump off. Last night I hadn't been thinking straight. And I refused to be played. No matter how hot the sex. It was about damned time. I had finally seen the light.

The universe must've acknowledged my realization because a blinding flash of light streaked through our vehicle as an echoing boom radiated beneath us. Followed by the overwhelming sounds of shots pelting the vehicle to our front.

The vehicle jostled us back and forth before coming to a stop. My lungs burned. I began to cough, and a sinking feeling dropped to the pit of my stomach.

High wails came from the occupants of the vehicle, and I froze. The uncertainty of what just happened caused my breath to catch. Though I had a pretty good idea.

Maya shrieked next to me. "What was that?"

It sounded like an IED explosion and the use of AK-47s. But I wasn't sure.

"I don't know." I spoke calmly, trying to reassure myself everything was okay more than pacify her. She had always been there for me. We took care of each other. The least I could do was keep her calm. Inside, I was shaking. But I wouldn't let that show. I took her hand in mine. "We're going to be fine, Maya," I whispered as I gripped her hand. She hunched down into my side, and I wrapped my arms around her, looking toward the hard plastic separating us from the driver and officer in the passenger seat. "Stay down." I lifted a fraction. The scene in front of me was a horror story.

The Humvees before us had exploded, and sand and clouds of smoke surrounded us. Definitely an IED. One big and powerful enough to take out two vehicles, leaving us vulnerable. "We've been attacked. I repeat, we've been attacked," the soldier on the passenger side barked into the radio communicating back to the base.

"Everybody stay down!" the driver instructed. His booming voice roared like I'd never heard before. Immediately after, both soldiers jumped out of the truck. And the roar of unmistakable gunshots pierced my ears. They came in a rapid succession.

Pop, pop, pop, pop.

Gunshots drowned out the shrieks of the girls. My breath labored, I couldn't make myself move. I watched in horror as local men shot at the vehicles from high above. With a white truck rushing down the mountain, weapons appearing from every opening of the vehicle. Maya yanked on my arm, urging me to hunch back down. The shimmer of white smoke and the rancid smell of gunpowder and death wafted in the air.

We were under attack.

The two soldiers shot back. Coming out of my trance, I dropped to the floor. "We'll be okay if we do as we were told." I tried to assure the rest of the girls and the director. My words were futile, but complete panicking was pointless. It would serve us no good if we wanted to survive. The incessant gunfire of the AK-47s assured me the massive bomb that had gone off had been the least of our problems.

Our nightmare was just beginning.

Gun power surrounded us. And the truck rocked viciously. The amount of time passing was irrelevant, whether seconds or minutes, it still felt as if years were taken off my life. My forehead throbbed, resembling one of the intense, pounding headaches accompanied by nausea, vision blurs, and debilitating pressure I experienced when I had the misfortune of having a migraine.

Our reality took center stage, the disorientation becoming a second thought as queasiness crawled up my throat. We were supposed to be safe. Kyle had given me his word—why hadn't *he* been on this convoy escorting us?

I refused to die scared. Maya held me with a death grip, and I grew defiant. I needed to know what was happening. I repeated my earlier action and peeked through the plastic divider, my gut clenching at what I saw, and I held my hand to my mouth. Blood, and our driver slumped over the shattered, bullet-pierced window. The bile working its way up my throat made a comeback. I was going to be sick.

I hunched back down, dragging in breath after breath. My mind raced, fighting the pain in my head as I got my wits together, attempting to control the nausea. We'd been targeted. Would the shooters kidnap a bunch of Americans and hold them for ransom? The political words "we don't negotiate with terrorists" ran through my head.

Through the chaos, I heard a haunting grunt and just knew the other solider had been killed. Maya whimpered at my side. It was deafening. She'd heard the grunt. Tears streamed down her face in droves, my own impending tears struggling to break free. She pulled at my arm again. "Sara, please."

I nodded. We huddled back on the floor of the vehicle. And my body shook anticipating what might happen next. At any second, men could burst in, killing us like they'd killed the soldiers. Perspiration broke out across my brows, cascading down into my eyes. They stung. I wiped at the sweat and momentarily gazed around in slow motion at the scared faces and our skimpy tank tops peeking from underneath our thin, tight jackets. And envisioned our possible outcome. Our apparel could anger some. We could be raped. I braced myself, holding onto Maya, and stared out the back of the truck. Through the fog, I saw the remaining Humvees had veered out, each to opposite sides, the soldiers surrounding the convoy. It almost looked like a tree's branches. They fired back at the enemies, and I grew wary of how any of the USO personnel could help. But before I could formulate any type of plan, the vehicle started moving.

My eyes watered and chills spread over the entire length of my body. This couldn't be happening, the transport was still on. I now saw the side profile of a swarthy man with a long beard driving the vehicle, his similar-looking wingman to his right. My heart grew heavy. They'd killed our protection. I couldn't help but think, were we next?

The rest of the girls were finally clued in on our looming future. Our terrified director no longer held her usual control. Her face had paled and she stared off at nothing in particular. A reluctant hush filled the air, and we all became silent, less the muffled sobs.

I closed my eyes and did something I hadn't done for years.

I prayed.

I gave a short prayer for the soldiers whose Humvees had exploded. Then the driver and passenger. They'd made the ultimate sacrifice. And I prayed for Kyle to come for me, and rescue us, to tap into his spiritual side and be guided in his path toward me. Not as my lover, or my boyfriend, or even my friend, but as the only man who I trusted and believed could save us now.

11

KYLE

An hour after the convoy left, the first chilling call came through the radio. We'd been tuned into the channels communicating with each vehicle on the convoy. SEALs were considered elite and didn't do these types of convoys. Instead, we were on the QRF; quick response force.

I lowered the weapon I was cleaning in my compound and listened as a soldier shouted that they were under attack. The hairs on the back of my neck immediately stood on end. I didn't want to be right. My gut had tried to warn me, and I had ignored it. God damn it.

The radio grew quiet. Shit. That was a bad sign. When a convoy was attacked, whenever possible soldiers were trained to stop the convoy and move the vehicles out to the sides to remove themselves from the danger zone. Soldiers that weren't hit were to get out of the vehicles and assume defense fighting positions. It was their way of surrounding the convoy, forming a barrier of people with weapons. Each vehicle had a radio running on the same frequency communicating with the base. The fact that we'd only received one call and it had been dropped told me those soldiers had to vacate the vehicles to eradicate the attackers. Fuck.

I tightened my loud bearing vest and looked over to Pat, Vic, and the rest of my fire Team. "Load 'em up." No other words were exchanged, it wasn't needed. We were expected to be quick-witted, trained to move at a moment's notice, and that's what we did just then. We began to collect our weapons when the second call came in.

"The USO convoy was ambushed. A roadside bomb has disabled two vehicles. The medics still on board will assess the damage and provide immediate medical attention to as many as possible. We were under heavy enemy fire. There are casualties. We also have a hostage situation. The first troop carrier containing the USO guests was taken. The driver and officer on board were killed. We need immediate backup." That was the vehicle Sara was in. The look on my face clued the guys in to my thoughts.

"You don't know what happened, man," Pat stated sympathetically. He knew I was thinking about Sara. I nodded, removing the fucked-up thought from my head. My thought process was warped with anguish and I had to be positive. With the help of my Team, we loaded our weapons and sprinted back to our command. A quick briefing was conducted before our forty-man Team took off. My eight-man fire squad, which consisted of myself, Vic, Pat, Grant, Mitch, Shane, Erik, and Joaquín, led the convoy.

As swiftly as we could, we climbed into the first available Humvee, the up-armored metal camouflaging our surroundings. Luckily the vehicles were checked daily so finding ready-to-go Humvees was never a problem. Each vehicle contained four SEALs. I sat in the front passenger seat in the foremost vehicle, wanting the first opportunity at destroying our enemy. The vehicles couldn't have moved any faster—we shot out of the base like bats out of hell, gunning it down the road. Our vehicles sped through the desert on the path the convoy had taken. Roadside bomb, my ass. Sure we had them all the time, but my gut told me this was no random attack. These Americans had been taken for a reason, to be made examples of. Soon enough we'd find out what we were dealing with.

Pat saw it first. "Fuck, man."

Passing another mountainside hill, we approached the convoy, and a few soldiers waved at our incoming vehicles. Strewn on the side of the road, in the midst of a sand storm, were over a dozen bodies. The damage inflicted was ghastly. Soldiers, American men. All brutally shot, each one missing their weapons. No matter how many times we'd gone through this, it never got easier.

Joaquín, our driver, stopped the Humvee. At the drop of a hat, Vic, Grant, and Shane jumped out first—they were Corpsmen and the best equipped to handle the situation. If there was any chance they could save one soldier, then their assistance would be worth it.

I turned and gave the surrounding area a once-over, assessing my perimeters. Staring up at the steep mountains, I immediately recognized the path the assailants had used to attack. These bastards had executed their plan to perfection, outnumbering the soldiers. By blowing up the first two vehicles, the fire power raining down from the mountains had taken the rest of the men off guard. It must have taken seconds. And within minutes, they'd driven off with an entire cheerleading squad and one of our fucking vehicles.

I exited the Humvee. Pat, Mitch, Joaquín, Erik, and I followed shortly behind the Corpsmen, our guns scanning the landscape, looking for targets. Following the briefing instructions we'd had back at the base, each man got to work. Some checked the area and others spoke to the surviving soldiers, getting any intel that would be helpful. The medics provided medical attention and assisted the horrified athletes and their coach.

Shane stood to my side and checked one of the soldiers' pulse as Vic and Grant tended to the other nearby men.

"Dead." My heart ached.

"Same here," Vic announced.

"Fuck." I knelt beside one of the men, closed his eyes, and prayed over his body. I wasn't a chaplain, but being a reverend's son compelled me to pray for his salvation, despite my faith being constantly tested at war.

A SEAL pointed to the same tire tracks I'd seen. "The vehicles were definitely ambushed. The perpetrators came down that side of the mountain." He pivoted, signaling down the road. "And followed that path. There must be a village close by."

"For sure this was a targeted attack," Vic added. "The girls could be anywhere. One hundred bucks says the troop carrier was abandoned somewhere up the road. It's too risky for them to be seen in it. And if you check the top of those mountains, you'll see tire tracks going whichever which way. The rest of those motherfuckers hightailed it back into one of the villages or hidden caves."

I simply nodded. I didn't need to speak. He was right. We'd done this enough not to know what happened. I needed to gather my thoughts, and as the squad leader plan of action with my men.

I glanced around at my squad, every part of me filling with pride. I was in charge of the best SEALs. We respected and believed in each other. If anyone could save these women, we could. And we would.

I started walking in the direction of the remaining troop carrier, praying along the way. I knew how frightened the girls must've been. I prayed to be guided to them, to Sara. And let me honor my word of keeping her safe.

I approached the troop carrier and first spoke to the coach. The elderly man wore a somber expression. The many creases surrounding his sunken eyes and flat-lined, quivering lips seemed to deepen by the second. He reminded me of my Pops. Though I'd never seen my Pops this scared. Most of the players wore the same expression. As big as they were, understandably, the players were overwhelmed and had plenty of questions. I assured them all their questions would be answered when they were safely back on base. After directing a good portion of the Team to finish attending to the players and provide medical attention to whomever necessary, my men loaded the fallen soldiers. This was one of the hardest parts of the job. The body count was more than we anticipated, and it hurt like hell each time we loaded another fallen soldier.

Once everyone was loaded and secured, the convoy took off back to the base. We rode in silence. Out of respect for the lives lost, and out of hope that we'd be able to save the other innocent Americans who had been taken by terrorists when their desire had been simply to entertain us.

I often felt that the public saw us SEALs as killers, as sadistic psychos who enjoyed killing. But seeing war, seeing innocent lives taken filled me with rage. Fuck yeah, I wanted to kill. I wanted to kill the motherfuckers who'd murdered in cold blood these innocent men. The purposely ruthless and unfeeling manner in which their lives had ended was hard to swallow. These were sons, fathers, and husbands who would never come home to their families. The same motherfuckers who took great joy in taking innocent women would pay. Make no mistake, I wanted their blood on my hands.

I'd promised Sara I would keep her safe. And I intended to keep that promise. Whoever took her took the wrong girl. Because I would tear this country apart to find her.

This was exactly why I'd left football.

I'd never win MVP, never win a championship ring, but some heroes don't play games.

12

SARA

The minutes agonizingly dragged on as the truck barreled down the road. The more time that passed, the more hopeless everyone became. Little by little, being helpless chipped away at me. We had been living on a knife's edge since the truck had taken off. The whimpers of my friends could barely be heard over the engine. We'd broken off in pairs, holding the other. Maya and I huddled together, praying. I kept telling her I knew Kyle and his Team would find us, but internally I was losing my nerve. My heartbeat raced, my limbs shook, and my stomach knotted. With each bump on the road, the contents of my last meal swished in my stomach in a bubbling, boiling mess. Our cellphones had lost reception as soon as we'd left the base. Many lost power. I'd asked a teammate the time. Found out they'd been driving an hour. We rode deep into the mountains. Landmarks looked the same, making it difficult to decipher where we were. My mind worked overtime. Long hours of watching too much television contributed in playing havoc with my thoughts. I wrung my hands to prevent them from shaking. Tugged my ears when the ringing prevented me from hearing their path. These terrorists could be taking us anywhere, maybe they planned to rape us, or behead us on live television. Almost worse than the thought of dying was imagining my mother watching her baby girl's throat be slit by some sadist. The thought sickened me. Scared me to my core. The fear filling my lungs till I gasped for air. My trembling breath mixed with a quiet sob.

The vehicle slowed to a stop, and terror gathered in my belly. It felt like the rapid descent of a roller coaster crashing into the ground. My chest wall ached with the rattling pace in which my heart pounded. We were at mercy of these insurgents.

Maya clutched my hand harder, her skin clammy.

The ignition became silent. Doors opened and shut. Then a man with wiry hair and crazy eyes came into view at the back of the vehicle, an AK-47 with a ton of ammo wrapped around his chest.

Kyle... Where are you?

I stared at the grubby man. What were the motives of our captors? Ransom? Exchange? Or perhaps to humiliate and punish immodest American women.

The crazy-eyed man scanned the back of the truck with his weapon. His erratic movements controlled every shallow breath I released.

"Mobiles!" he boomed in broken English, waving the weapon like a flag.

We tossed our phones onto the floor of the vehicle. For a second, I allowed myself to believe that we were just getting robbed. Yes they had murdered the soldiers, but maybe the terrorists just wanted the vehicle and their weapons. It was clear my mind was playing tricks on me, holding onto false hope.

But my gut told me my ridiculous theory was nothing more than wishful thinking.

I heard the roar of engines and for a beat hope filled me,

returned with a powerful vengeance. Was it our rescuers? Please.

No. A bunch of swarthy men entered our vehicle, each branding an AK-47. The weapons served their purpose of intimidation.

Snatched by the back of our necks, we got pushed off the truck. Crazy Eyes chose me to grab. The stench of his grimy hand revolted me. Trying to free myself from his hold, I lost my footing and fell to the ground, taking Maya with me. "Oof." I winced. Dirt had kicked up when I met the ground. I could taste it.

"Up!" Crazy Eyes barked. My eyes narrowed, and I wiped my knees and helped Maya to stand. We were marched away from the truck in pairs, the ten of us outnumbered by our captors. No matter how we were dressed, I felt naked.

I held onto Maya. There was no way in hell I was letting go of her hand. At the moment, she was my lifeline. My mouth was parched from the heat as I focused on three beaten-up trucks, mud splashed on the exterior. The men didn't waste any time. We were split into two groups of three and one of four, and I felt some solace knowing I had Maya for comfort. We were separated randomly, depending on who we stood by. Denise, our director, was to my left, and became the third hostage in our group being led to the proposed new transportation. At first we kept our heads down and did as we were told. I got the feeling they didn't want us looking directly at them too much. And I for one didn't want to cause any uproar. Denise clearly didn't feel the same. We'd almost made it to the truck when she dug her heels into the ground, refusing to take another step. Making an abrupt stop, I stood at her back and gave her a little nudge, willing her to move. "I refuse to walk to my death. I won't give them the satisfaction."

"Walk!" the bigger of the two terrorists ordered, his hot breath singeing my neck.

"No," she uttered rebelliously. My heart sank. Why was she doing this? Now was not the time to be difficult. All hope was not lost. It was small, at times seeming microscopic, but it was there. I believed that. I had to.

Maya jumped when the men dug their weapons into our backs. We pushed forward but Denise wouldn't budge. She was strong in her convictions, that I knew. I experienced it every day. But more than that, she was stubborn. Set in her ways.

"Walk!" they ordered again, this time much louder. The muscles in my legs ached. My body shuttered.

"Denise, please," Maya implored, her voice barely above a whisper. She was ignored. I'd never seen her look so scared. Maya was a tough cookie, but this type of vexatious predicament could break even the strongest person.

In the distance, doors shut. The rumbling of engines ensued. The other trucks took off with our friends. And I wondered if I'd ever see them again or if we'd all be taken to different places. Just then one of the two men grabbed Denise, seizing her head by the roots of her short hair. She let out a pained screech.

"WALK!" He bared his teeth, letting out a deep grunt from the back of his throat. The rotten choppers were full of decay. I was certain the man had never seen a dentist a day in his life.

She surprised everyone when she turned and spat at his face. The angry man retaliated by backhanding her, practically foaming, the corners of his mouth retaining the mass of small bubbles like a rabid dog. Her head reared back with the impact and simultaneous gasps left our lips at her bloodied cheek. She looked back at the assailant and was unrecognizable. Rage taking over, a storm brewed in her eyes. *Please don't do something stupid.* It was too late. Advancing on him, she was shot, the sequence of hot bullets piercing her chest.

I drank salty tears as the thug behind me pushed us forward with his weapon. Denise's sudden death traumatized Maya and

I had to haul her beside me, clutching her to my body like a child held a rag doll. I didn't allow myself to look back. Couldn't stomach the thought of getting another glimpse at our dead director. My heart hurt too damned much. This wasn't happening. It couldn't be. It had to be a bad dream.

Crammed in the sweaty vehicle, I had the burden of being placed immediately to the right of the driver, the barrel of his weapon an inch from my thigh. We started to drive. I couldn't help thinking that one more pothole, one more unearthed bomb, and that rifle could go off and blast a hole through my leg or kill any one of us. The more I tried to push the thought out of my head, the more I fixated on it. Was this how we would die? Would we meet our maker like Denise had? Then be abandoned like roadkill. I thought of her body rotting before being discovered and swallowed back a fresh bout of bile.

The crazy-eyed driver said something in a language I didn't understand, but I didn't need to be fluent in his native tongue. His words, the motions of his rifle translated into any language.

The hours passed down the sandy road, the four of us confined in the same stench-filled space, and we were transferred to other vehicles at least three other times. Same routine, same driver, another mud-stained vehicle, the identical pinch of the AK-47 across his lap, its barrel at my side. Maya stayed silent, as did I. Affliction accompanied our every move. Tried to keep myself sane with thoughts of my family, desperately tethering myself to happy memories.

As the day dragged into night, my sense of self and grip on reality began to loosen. Nothing I had accomplished in my life mattered to these kidnappers. I was no longer a woman, someone's daughter. I was nothing more than a possession to be used for these men to get what they wanted.

The only problem was I didn't have a clue what that was.

13

KYLE

"We've got every man on this, Lieutenant Commander Lawson. Drones are being sent out now, and we have Osprey helicopters surveying the terrain. We will find them."

I nodded while clutching the phone but my gut doubted the words of my Rear Admiral. He was the best the military had. Admiral Stevens had orchestrated some of the best rescues in military history. I was honored to serve with him.

In reality, we didn't know who took the women, why they took them, and where they were. No group had taken responsibility for the kidnappings, yet. I had my theories—the usual suspects—religious fundamentalists, radicals, terrorists. But I never wasted my time on conjecture; my decisions were made on facts, not guesses. My actions could mean life or death to these women—the gravity of the predicament and responsibility weighed heavily on my soul.

"Thank you, sir. I'd like to be on the ground and have my Team be the first ones embedded when we discover their location."

"Roger that. I'll update you when I hear anything new."

My first decision had been to return with my Team to base to formulate a plan, gather intelligence, and call in air support. There was absolutely no time to be spent on a wild goose chase. This wasn't Hollywood—I wasn't miraculously going to find her by the side of the road.

Since the abduction, thousands of military personnel, both Stateside and in-country were working on this. For now, I could do little more than be prepared and wait.

I grinded my teeth. The word burned. Wait. Safe on base, with a television, a computer, food, and my military family.

I paced around the room. Every second that clicked on the clock grated at my nerves. Anger and worry consumed me.

Pat placed his hand on my shoulder. "I get it. It's personal. This is exactly how I felt when I'd left Annie in the brothel. But I found her. We're going to find Sara."

I shook his hand off. I didn't need his comfort—I needed to take action.

Ten more agonizing minutes passed. Finally, the phone rang.

"Lawson, a terrorist group has taken responsibility for the kidnappings. The girls' faces are plastered all over the media."

I clicked on the computer—pictures of the squad, numbered as if for execution. Their director was noticeably missing. Running a hand down my face, I studied Sara's face intently, her beautiful blue eyes, her angelic smile. Rubbed across my chest. This fucking hurt. I would never forgive myself if I couldn't save her.

I'd always believed I was put on this earth for a purpose—save lives to make up for the ones taken.

Sara was my duty, my mission. I would rescue her or die trying.

14

SARA

I'd completely lost track of time, as the never-ending landscape of desert mountains rolled past the window throughout the day. Now the sky was dark. I tuned out most sounds except for Maya's. Her sobs had stopped. She grew quiet as the truck seemed to slow down.

I clutched the armrest as Crazy Eyes stopped the vehicle. Where were we? I quickly glanced around, hoping to see some type of nearby shelter, or at least the other vehicles behind us.

But there was nothing.

We were alone.

The dark of night, the dust of the desert, imposing mountains and trails, and the smell of diesel were the only elements surrounding us. I felt small in comparison. It was the feeling of being swallowed whole. I wanted to close my eyes and be back home. End this nightmare.

Crazy Eyes chuckled when my breath caught as the barrel of the AK-47 belonging to his accomplice pressed into my left shoulder from the backseat. "Walk."

It took me a moment to understand the word walk even though it was spoken in English. Walk? Walk where?

In the non-sound of silence, I realized the answer.

To the middle of nowhere in the desert mountains. To the dead of night. Unmarked. Untraceable.

Where we would never be found.

I stepped out and clutched Maya's hand as she exited the vehicle. Her hand was ice-cold.

Why would they take us here? There could only be one reason.

We were going to be assassinated. Just like Denise. Only the lewd looks in their eyes told me we'd be raped first.

Maya turned to me, and though I could barely make out her face in the mask of night, I knew by her quaking voice she was terrified. I'd grown numb. "Sara, if we go out there, we will be killed."

On a daily basis, Maya took care of me. Cared for me like a big sister. It was my turn to be the stronger one. I put my arm around her and whispered in her ear, "If they kill us now, they can't use us for leverage. We're in for a long night. We were probably sixty miles from the military base when we were taken. I'm sure Kyle is on his way. That's why the other girls aren't with us now. I'm sure they've already been saved."

But I didn't believe any of my words. Not a single one.

Neither did Maya.

Her voice choked with impending sobs. "I don't want to die."

I made a conscious decision at that point. I refused to focus on being certain I was about to die. I would savor the time I had left. And protect Maya at all costs.

We continued to march deeper into the night, the walls of darkness closing in on us. Soft lighting came from a small flashlight one carried. When I turned back, glancing over my shoulder, I made out Crazy Eyes and his friend speaking in hushed voices, both their rifles with extra ammunition pointed at us.

There was no way out, no escape. They noticed I was staring and became silent. I whipped my head forward so fast it ached.

"I can still see the truck. We're not far," I whispered to myself. I racked my brain with a plan. I wouldn't be discarded on the side of the road. Left to decompose. I refused. We walked in unison, at first no sounds but their heavy footsteps behind us. They were in horrible shape and I heard their heavy breathes as we marched. We didn't have weapons but maybe we could outrun them.

Then we stopped. Still in the middle of nowhere. I analyzed the area, looking for a way out.

That was when Crazy Eyes removed a knife from one of his pants leg pockets, its blade lightly shinning under the stars above.

It wasn't just any knife.

Not a long blade that could execute us in a single swipe, more of a butcher knife. I wondered if they relished in slow torture. If they planned to saw our heads off, gradually, agonizingly, making us suffer for as long as possible.

The other thug kicked the back of my leg, then Maya's. Her knees buckled, and I held onto her, plastering her to my side. "Get on your knees and turn away from us." The bastard knew more English than he had let on.

Maya burst into tears. And it took all my strength not to give these heathens the satisfaction of my terror.

I looked up to the moon for comfort, but even the moon had failed me. Had hidden when I needed it. But the stars lit up the sky.

The same stars Kyle and I made love under the night before.

And at that moment, I made a vow.

A vow to live. To believe.

Because I knew that somewhere out there Kyle was under

those same stars, and they would lead him to me. I just needed to figure out how to keep us alive until then.

15

KYLE

No word, no calls, no new intel. Where the fuck could they be? I was so desperate it had even crossed my mind to go rogue, but I wasn't stupid. I had to trust the military intelligence. A dumbass decision like that would most likely end up with Sara dying and maybe even some of my men, not to mention me losing my career. But at the moment I only had one thing on my mind. My only goal was to find Sara, alive, and the best shot of that was to go through the appropriate channels. I had faith in my commanders, the United States Navy, and God. I knew what needed to be done.

Finally, when the stars lit up the sky and my sense of helplessness had penetrated deep within me, my phone rang. I recognized my admiral's voice as he spoke into the receiver.

"Lieutenant Commander Lawson, we've spotted the vehicles abandoned by a side road. A drone has taken a picture of the hostages in the desert. Airstrike is out of the question with American hostages. Assemble your Team for a night op." The tone in his voice was reassuring, hopeful. My confidence rose—I was going to find them. Out here every minute counted, and I breathed out a deep sigh of relief that hostages had been spotted. She was alive. She had to be.

I made notes while my commanding officer laid out the plan. God was on my side—tonight was a new moon, but he would guide the way. The sky would be black, perfect night for an operation. We would fly in on a C-130, parachute into the night, and then take foot. Once we surrounded the area, we would destroy the terrorists and save the hostages. A typical day at the office. I wasn't even scared, I was excited. In my mind, there was no chance of failure. I'd done versions of this operation before. Enough times to know what to expect. One day these thugs would realize there was nowhere to run, nowhere to hide. If they fucked with Americans, we would find them, and we would kill them. We were the best. And there was nothing that fired us up more than protecting our own. Only the lowest of the low took pleasure in hurting women.

The pounding in my chest ebbed and a fire took its place. Calm, measured, and ready to burn anything that stood in its path. I made my way to the barracks and awoke my Team. Being fresh and ready to go was a given, yet I hadn't slept a wink. After a quick briefing we checked out weapons, and headed to the C-130. Vic had his Team dog, Cuervo, with him. Cuervo was a badass Belgian Malinois. That dog could sense the enemy before we could, skydive, and had captured more men than I had. He truly was man's best friend.

Just as we finished loading up, Pat took me aside and placed his hand on my shoulder. "You have that look about you, brother. I know you can feel it just as much as me. We'll find her. We found Annie and we didn't even know where she was. Piece of cake. You understand?"

Nodding, I pulled him in for a hug, and he didn't resist. We were closer than close. Swim buddies at BUD/S. It didn't matter back then that I was an officer and he was enlisted. Our color, our backgrounds, neither meant a thing. It didn't matter that I was rich and he was poor. That I had a college degree and he had a high school education. How many nights had we huddled together trying to stay warm in the cold ocean water during surf torture? He was my brother.

But Pat was a married man now, a father of one, and soon-to-be two kids. The weight of his new responsibilities weighed heavily on me. I would not make Annie a widow—she'd most certainly been through enough. I would not leave their children without a father. If this mission failed, it was on me. I had promised Annie I would keep him safe, and I never break my promises. Not to Pat, not to Annie, not to Vic, and definitely not to Sara. You weren't shit if you couldn't keep your word.

I kept shaking my head, letting him know I understood as we hugged it out before Mitch, Shane, Grant, Joaquín, Erik, Vic, and Cuervo climbed into the C-130, and Pat and I quickly followed. As the aircraft took off, I focused on the stars in the sky. With the absence of the moon, they seemed brighter than normal.

I bowed my head and prayed. I thanked God for this mission, and asked him to protect her until I could do it myself.

16

SARA

Time stood still as the rocks dug into my knees. This was it, the last moments of my life. I'd never get married, I'd never have kids. I was only twenty-one and I was sure I was about to be slayed.

The steel metal of the blade pressed against the back of my neck. Maya screamed and he pointed the knife at her.

But he wasn't done with me yet. I'd moved and that only made him angrier. He yanked my hair back in one meaty fist as if in a high ponytail, pulling the strands so tight my scalp burned. As he twisted my hair, his grip tightened, and I was certain he was preparing to behead me. He raised the knife and I let out a bloodcurdling scream when the blade sliced through the air.

Within seconds the tension released from my head.

But I was alive.

I cranked my head back and saw Crazy Eyes laughing, holding my hair in his hand. His rotting teeth were yellow, the stench from his mouth repulsing me when he lowered to wave the hair in my face. Then he spat at my face.

I wiped at the thick saliva running down my face and ran

my fingers through what was left of my hair. I'd been shorn like a sheep. Maya whimpered beside me as the other assailant looked on, enjoying the show. The sadistic storm brewing in his eyes told me the sick bastard was getting off on petrifying us.

Tears burned as they cascaded over my skin, but I forced myself to stop. They wouldn't see me cry. Crazy Eyes' stench filled the air as his hand wrapped around my neck. And I gulped trying to breath. Opening my eyes wide, I stared back at him.

My head jerked when he unzipped my jacket, the fabric ripping too easily, and I shook my head to say no. Please...no. He went for my arm next and I thought he would slice through it as well. He didn't. I flinched. He was instilling fear in me by slowly dragging the sharp blade and slicing through the material of the sleeve and stuffing the ripped material in my mouth. The tip of the blade then sliced my tank top, exposing my bra, and I gasped, dropping the material from my mouth. He instantly looked displeased.

My mouth clapped shut, and I bit my trembling lip, my mouth filled with a bitter metal taste. He paused and stared at my breasts then closed the small distance between us, nuzzling his head on my neck and then taking a single long lick between my cleavage before roughly squeezing one. A gag built in my throat, my body shaking as he released my breast. "Stand up!"

Hauling me to my feet, he placed the knife's handle in his mouth and grinned. His hands jerked as he pulled down my sweat pants over my hips, revealing my panties, leaving the sweat pants to bunch at my ankles above my sneakers. I considered struggling, fighting, kicking him in the groin, but his blade kept me at bay. He held it close enough to pierce my skin if need be. That and I heard the deep breaths his partner made. If I moved, one of them would tackle me to the ground and make me pay. I shivered when the cool air assaulted my exposed skin.

He ran a single finger down the center of my panties then

cupped my crotch, and my body convulsed. Not only would I be killed, but I'd be raped first. Rapid breaths of clipped air traveled from my lungs and out of my mouth, making me dizzy.

But then he dropped me back on the dirt and stood up straight, eyeing me like a farm animal at a state fair. Crazy Eyes adjusted his pants and he and his friend cackled. They took a few steps back from me and closer to Maya and I knew Maya was next. They were preparing to rape us. Maya looked like she wanted to run but Crazy Eyes kicked her and she fell to the ground.

She lay beside me, tears streaming down her dirt-covered face. I wanted to hug her. Tell her I loved her and how sorry I was I hadn't saved her. She was shaking in the cold, knowing we might only have seconds left before we were sexually tortured and then killed. Then I got the break I was desperately looking for. "You." Crazy Eyes' partner pointed his weapon at me. "Undress her." He stupidly turned after giving the command.

I grasped Maya's face in my hands. "Listen to me, we need to escape." I stared at the two men' backs then back at her and uttered softly, "I'm going to run, and they will both follow me. I can outrun them—I ran track in school. The dumbass left his keys in the ignition. Once they run after me, you are to run to the truck and drive. Do you understand me? Just drive into the night toward that town we passed. The SEALs will find you. They'll help you and then come for me."

"No. No way, Sara. I'm not leaving you. Besides, I'm not all that great in a crisis. Where would I drive? I'll be stuck in the middle of nowhere and get taken again. It's over, Sara. We're going to die here. I'm just glad we're not going to die alone."

I shook her, my eyes darting back to the men, who seemed to be plotting their next move. But it was so dark I couldn't figure out what it was.

"No. It's not over. Don't worry about me, I'll be fine. I ran long distance. I'll keep running or hide in some cave until Kyle finds me. I saw plenty of them on the drive here." I forced my voice to remain calm, so she wouldn't hear the fear in my words. I didn't believe the words I was saying to her. I was positive they would capture me, torture me, rape me, and behead me. But I wanted her to escape. A few years back Maya's oldest brother, Emilio, had been killed in a random gang-related drive-by shooting in Downtown LA. As expected, it had taken a toll on her parents, especially her father. Maya helped put her family back together and convinced them to move to San Diego. The love in her father's eyes for his children was something I used to long for with my own father. Until I grew up, sucked it up, and knew better. That same affection and warmth was how Maya took me under her wing when I moved to SD and tried out for the Wildfires. She became my family when I didn't have one near. And there wasn't anything I wouldn't do for family. Maybe I'd get lucky and come out unscathed. If I didn't, I'd made peace with it in my dying breath. Accepting and protecting my family meant a lot more than being a coward who disregarded their responsibilities, who turned their back and forgot what being a family meant. I wasn't anything like my father. Never was. Never would be. "We can do this. I'm going to run and they will follow me. I need you to run like the wind. Don't stop until you get to the truck. And don't stop driving until you get to that town a few miles away. Please, Maya. Trust me. The SEALs will find you."

Her breaths were rapid and she was shaking in my arms. "I won't. I won't go without you. We can run together. I need you, Sara. I love you. You are my best friend. You're my sister. I can't do this without you. I'm so scared." Fresh tears appeared on her face.

"Yes you can, and you will. You are stronger than you know. I love you, Maya." I choked back sobs and softly shoved her.

"It's okay. Go, Maya. Go. Before they come back. If I don't come home—"

"Don't say that. We're going to make it. I won't leave you if you don't believe you'll make it back, too. We're going to dance together again. This will all be a bad dream." Her hopeful eyes told me if I had any chance of saving her, I'd have to lie to my best friend.

"I didn't mean that. I'm positive I'll make it out. I wouldn't be proposing it if I didn't." Footsteps approached and I knew it was time. I only had moments to save my friend's life. I glanced back to make sure the men were both watching me. And they were. Their look of agitation that I hadn't undressed Maya was palpable as they grew near.

I hugged Maya one last time. "You run and you don't stop, okay?" She sniffed and nodded her head.

One, two, three. I took a deep breath and pulled my pants up then gripped my jacket closed in one clinched fist. In a matter of seconds, I said a final prayer and rose to a crouching position. Before I could lose my nerve, I sprinted into the night.

The night air blew cold on my skin and stifled my breaths, my feet pounding the dirt as I ran. The more I pushed the more my body hurt, but I wouldn't stop. I white-knuckled the jacket to my chest, my exposed arm hitting the wind. I could hear one of the men yelling in broken English and the thumps of their boots told me they were in pursuit. A sinking feeling told me they would catch me, and they'd definitely kill me.

But I ran as fast as my feet would go. Wind blew against my ears, and a sound resembling the inside of a seashell appeared. My long strides dug into the dirt, and the voice of my high school track coach rang in my head. "Run, Sara, run. Move it, kid!" But his voice was soon replaced by Kyle's soothing voice. *"I'll take care of you while you're here and make sure you're safe."* It was almost if he was running beside me.

A gunshot rang out, and I cut a sharp left. In the distance, the unmistakable sound of a diesel truck rumbled to life, the sound fading by the second.

Maya had made it. She would be safe. And if I died saving her, it would be worth it.

17

KYLE

Inside the C-130, I checked everyone's parachute and equipment on my Team. The aircraft contained three Teams, which would split up and jump at different locations just like the assailants had done according to the drone pictures we received before taking off. Greedily I'd chosen the small group containing two members, one fair-haired and the other a brunette. Maya and Sara stuck together like glue. That was where I'd find my blond bombshell. I was certain of it.

For most ops we would carry a satellite radio, but since this was a night-op we carried a radio, which had an encrypting technology to ensure the transmission was more secure.

"Thirty minutes!" I yelled. My men lined up and used the piss tube mounted on the wall. *Last chance, fellas.* Before we knew it, we were almost at our destination.

"Ten minutes."

Everyone scrambled around the ramp. Time flew by in a blur, which was just how I wanted it.

"Five minutes."

Vic strapped Cuervo to him. The dog's attention to detail

and dedication never ceased to amaze me. Like I said, that dog was a badass.

The ramp lowered and I couldn't hear shit. I used my hand signals to my brothers. I studied the ground through my night vision goggles to make sure we were on course based on the aerial map I'd studied. Every minute that passed that I didn't know if she was safe brought on a fresh wave of feelings I'd worked hard to keep hidden. I'd fallen for Sara and now I wouldn't stop till I found her. I should have been honest with her. I should have manned up and told her how I felt about her. Staying silent like a pussy was not the last image I wanted her to have of me. So I'd studied that map like if my life depended on it. Our pilots were the fucking best but I needed to find my girl so I didn't want to walk any farther than I had to. *My girl.* Fuck. That had a nice ring to it. I flashed my hand, making sure to spread my fingers and jerked my thumb to the right. The loadmaster relayed my directions to the pilot who adjusted the nose of the C-130 five degrees starboard.

The ramp light turned from red to green. It was go time.

I signaled to my men for the last time before we jumped. We were twelve thousand feet above ground and even though I'd jumped out of planes a hundred times before, I prayed to God that this jump wouldn't be my last.

Vic and Cuervo jumped first. I made sure all my men left the aircraft. Pinching my thumb and index finger together, I brought them to my mouth and pressed them against my lips and gave one final prayer then free fell into the air before the aircraft left with the other two Teams to their assigned destinations.

After a minute, I opened my parachute and glided under the canopy. A beautiful moment, flying through the sky. We were so in synch our parachutes were aligned as if we were creating a stairway to heaven. I turned on my night optical device as I descended to the ground, my men landing before me.

Perfect. Pat and Mitch grabbed their weapons and secured the area while the rest of us hid our chutes. Vic released Cuervo, who quickly ran in front of us.

The sky provided another gift for us. The light rain. The perfect weather to camouflage our movements. We split our Team into two groups, ensuring we took different routes to our targets. If one group failed, the other would complete the mission. We were motherfucking SEALs. We'd die trying before giving up. Vic, Pat, and Grant came with me. We traipsed slowly through the dirt, the mud sticking to our boots.

Cuervo ran back to Vic, signaling he'd heard something ahead. I heard it too. Diesel. A truck. Sara's captors were coming toward us.

I signaled and we stood in position, our weapons pointed ahead.

The headlights shone through my goggles as I prepared to shoot out the tires. But we had to be careful on gunfire, we didn't want them to kill the women.

I aimed, shooting twice above the driver's side front tire. Being shot from the front was enough to deter the vehicle's movement. Funny how being faced with the barrel of a gun at close range made you cooperate, even when you didn't want to. We approached the vehicle, and in my scope I could see a girl alone, no terrorists.

What the fuck? A few more steps and her face came into focus. It was Maya.

She screamed hysterically when she heard the weapon being shot, the shine from the vehicle blocking her sight of us.

And there was no sign of Sara.

No.

I ran to her as the others fanned out. "Maya, you're safe. Breathe. It's Kyle. Where's Sara?"

She flung herself at me, wrapping her hands around my neck. "She, she, they cut off her hair and ripped her clothes. They were going to rape us, but she told me to escape. She ran away from them so they would follow her and I ran to the truck. She saved my life. They already killed our director and dumped the body." That was why the drone pictures showed groups with what looked like bigger groups. I knew there was a reason Maya and Sara were alone. The anguish in her voice broke my heart. She feared her friend was dead as well. I wasn't going to give up that easily.

I needed her to start talking. "How many of them? How long ago was this? Did you drive straight here and not change direction?"

She sobbed and I radioed the other four guys from the Team. "T-two of them. About fifteen min-minutes. And yes, I stayed straight. She risked her life for me. Please. You have to find her. She saved me so I could find help."

And she had. I would find Sara. I'd been right all along. Sara was more than a pretty face. She was a fighter. A survivor. A savior. Just like me.

Mitch, Joaquín, Shane, and Erik arrived, our Team complete. Shane examined Maya who was surprisingly unharmed. Her chest heaved up and down as she sobbed but no bruises that I could see. We radioed for air support and one by one, those men stayed with her until they all could be extracted. Having her continue on would only slow us down and put her in further danger.

Their mission was over. Maya had been saved. But my girl was out there. Somewhere. Alone in the night.

I signaled to Pat, Vic, and Grant. Fifteen minutes, at least ten miles, though I doubted Maya had been driving sixty miles an hour.

I briefed my men. "Sara is still out there. At least ten miles due north, following the tracks of the vehicle. Start moving.

We're not going to stop until we find her. Gentlemen, it's going to be a long night."

18

SARA

The stomp of their boots in pursuit of me shook the earth, ringing in my ears like a repetitive bad dream. My shins burned but I pushed through the pain, running for my life. I had a bit of a lead on them since they weren't in the best shape, but that lead was shrinking by the second. They were going to hunt me down like an animal and shred me to pieces. Breathing hurt. Hell, everything hurt. I wanted the dirt to open up, create a hiding place for me, swallow my body until they passed. Still, I kept going. The stars illuminated a mountain in the distance. If only I could make it to that mountain, I would have a chance. I could shield myself until they gave up finding me. But even if I succeeded, would I succumb to the elements? Would I be able to be rescued? It was a chance I had to take. I wouldn't forgive myself if I didn't try. I would not die freely.

My strides grew bigger. All those months training to be a cheerleader had been worth it. I flashed back to my daily runs on the track at SDSU, complaining about the heat messing up my hair, or the harsh sun on my skin. Every run I had made prepared me for this dash of my life. My pace was steady and fast. These men surely couldn't be in as good shape as I was.

They were medium built; some would say thin. But they lacked muscle and endurance. Their only advantage was their lungs were used to the high altitudes and mine were most surely not. I was spoiled by the San Diego sunshine and the crisp sea-level air. I forced myself to breathe through my fear and kept running. I was used to the long distance. It was what I excelled at in track.

As I ran, a false sense of security passed over me. They would never catch me, I would be able to hide out and await rescue, these fools would never take me alive. I psyched myself up for the race of my life.

The sound of their boots faded and I was more confident in my victory. I could see the base of the mountain ahead and a few feet farther back appeared to be some type of cave. A few more steps, a few more breaths and I would make it. I was thin enough to blend in, or at least I hoped so.

My left foot pounded into the ground and without warning I heard a terrible crack. My ankle gave out under me and I collapsed onto the dirt.

A sharp pain radiated through my body. I was so close. I summoned every ounce of strength and pulled myself to my feet. Not now. Not when I was so close to safety.

Dammit—that goddam rock had now cost me precious seconds. I hobbled forward, my pace slowed, willing myself to just keep running, no matter how great the pain. The irony dawned on me that a day ago this injury would've gutted me for potentially ruining my dancing career, yet now my only concern was saving my life, even if there was permanent damage. How trivial my former concerns seemed to me now.

A few more paces and I could hear the rhythm of the boots getting closer.

A gun shot rang out into the night. I instinctively dodged, praying the bullet wasn't flying toward me.

No, I can do this. I will make it. I won't be taken.

I could feel him behind me. Closer, so close his hot breath blew on my neck. No!

Whack!

The back of a gun smacked me across the head, instantly knocking me to the ground. My head ached like crazy. But that was the least of my problems.

"You whore!" Crazy Eyes barked.

He pointed the gun to my head. I had no choice. I wanted to live. And I would do anything to survive. If I kept him talking I could buy myself more time, and maybe a bit of sympathy.

"No, please," I begged, forcing myself to kneel in front of him. "I'm sorry. Please, don't kill me. I promise I'll be good. I'll behave."

The crushing pain in my head enveloped my body. And the pressure in my ankle shot straight up my leg. But I refused to cry.

"Please!" I reached out and grabbed his leg. "I'm yours. I'll do as you say. I'll do anything you ask."

19

KYLE

I informed Pat, Vic, and Grant about our plan as Vic held onto Cuervo, who was ready to go. "It would take us an hour or more to get to her by foot. We're going to take the truck until we are a mile out and then walk."

The four of us piled into the truck after Cuervo and headed straight back to where Maya had come from. Where Sara was. Where those terrorists were holding her hostage. Where I hoped I'd find her alive. My concern in taking the truck was that these motherfuckers would hear the vehicle, maybe assassinate Sara as we approached. But Maya had said she had driven for fifteen minutes. It would take us an hour to reach that location by foot. I couldn't, and wouldn't risk Sara's life. I needed to get to her now.

Pat drove the truck as the rest of us scanned the landscape with our weapons. Searching for something, anything that would lead us to Sara. I doubted these psychos had night-vision goggles, and their plans had been compromised, especially when they had been foolish enough to allow Maya to escape. But the night held its secrets tight—no flickers of lights, no movement of other vehicles, no sounds of gunfire.

The minutes passed and the sound of Sara's voice rang in my head. I prayed for a sign, a signal, something to bring me to her.

Pop!

Pat cut the engine before I even asked him to. My prayers had been answered. The unmistakable pop of a rifle. Someone was near. Adrenaline spiked through my body. Had those motherfuckers killed Sara? For a mere second I felt the pit of stomach drop so far I thought I could deposit it out of my ass. But the determination I had driving through my veins was a hell of a lot stronger. I shook the thought out of my head.

I signaled to exit the truck and the four of us fanned out across the landscape, with Cuervo leading the pack to our front. I focused my night vision goggles but couldn't see a damned thing yet. We were too far out. Despite the best image intensification and thermal fusion technology in the world, I couldn't see shit. I had Pat, the best sniper, on my side. And our secret weapon, Cuervo, would smell these motherfuckers before we could spot them.

The night remained motionless and I still couldn't detect the origin of the gunshot. But my goggles focused in on a patch of disturbed earth in the distance. I signaled my men and we approached.

There, in a small pile, was fabric from clothes. Sara's clothes. A sliced piece of a jacket that she had been wearing the last time I'd seen her. And her blonde locks mixed in the dirt.

My hands shook. They were fucking animals. They'd chopped off her hair—what would they do next? I scoured the earth for blood, praying I would find none. Cuervo's nose must have picked up their scent and he ran in front of Vic. That a boy.

A wave of relief washed over me. "No blood."

The words echoed in my head. *No blood.* They had just cut her hair, humiliated her. Images filled my mind—Sara being raped, these vile motherfuckers violating her, grabbing her flesh, forcing their dicks in her mouth, inside her. Since I'd become a SEAL, I'd seen more brutality than I ever wished to recall in my lifetime. But the images of children and women being defiled had always been the hardest ones for me to reconcile. At night, those visuals haunted my nightmares—their screams filled my head. I had been unable to save them.

But not tonight. Tonight's mission would be a success. I was more certain than I had been about anything in my life. She was the reason I left my career, though I hadn't known it at the time. Meeting Sara at the bar last summer, seeing her on the USO tour, all of these events had led me to this moment. I was put on this earth to save her. And no motherfucker would stop me.

Stay strong just a little bit longer, baby. We're breathing the same air.

20

SARA

My tactic had worked. Crazy Eyes and his friend, who had joined him a few minutes after I'd been hit over the head with the rifle, seemed to be even more turned on by my defiance and sudden pleading.

And I'd been right about one thing—I had seen a cave in the distance. But I had thought that the cave would be my refuge. Instead, it was about to be my prison.

The barrel of the gun, now held by the friend, was placed at the back of my neck as Crazy Eyes led me to the cave. I didn't resist, my ankle was throbbing and the wound on my head made me dizzier than before. At this point, the only way out I could see was going along with whatever these two terrorists wanted, and praying that I was rescued soon. I'd made it farther than I'd anticipated. And Maya had made it out. Maybe I would, too. I looked around for any sign of another vehicle, a backup, but saw none. Or maybe at some point if they both passed out, I could kill them, but that was wishful thinking.

We arrived at the cave, and his friend took out a lighter and lit a lantern, which gave the cave a soft glow. It looked like the inside of a really fucked-up haunted house. Crazy Eyes licked his lips and motioned for me to sit and I complied. He pressed me back against the dirt and I closed my eyes. I didn't want to see his face as he raped me. If it saved me, I'd deal with the aftershock later the best I could. The physical pain would be enough of a reminder for the rest of my life, but maybe, if I could block out the image of being penetrated by this monster, I could someday recover.

A harsh sting flushed across my jaw and the sound and impact of a slap forced my eyes open. Crazy Eyes was now holding his erect pencil thin dick, pointing at it, as if I was supposed to be turned on. A wave of nausea rippled along my throat and threatened to get out.

He motioned for me to lower my pants and I did. His friend stood outside the cave, but instead of pointing his gun toward the land, he kept his eyes locked on me. Sick motherfucker wanted to watch. The way he stared at me like I would be used then discarded of filled me with terror.

I inhaled. I'd been wrong. I wasn't going to get saved. I was going to be raped and then slaughtered. Kyle hadn't come for me. None of the SEALs had. I would spend the last minutes of my life in pure agony.

Crazy Eyes leaned into me, closer and closer until our bodies touched. His chapped lips met mine and as much as I wanted to bite his lips and tongue off, I reminded myself that his friend had a gun, and I was already in enough pain. His hand made its way down my body and his finger pressed into my panties. My face contorted. His other hand reached and grabbed my breast, and I held my breath. Just when I thought I was seconds away from being raped he collapsed on me, blood splattering everywhere.

What the fuck?!

I screamed and noticed his friend was slumped over in the entrance of the cave, his head deformed, brains splattered.

I continued to scream, my lungs burning, my voice making

sounds I didn't know I was capable of making. My head spun from side to side, completely unable to comprehend what was happening.

A few seconds later, a dog strapped with military gear bounded up to me. And that's when I realized what had just happened.

I blinked back through my tears and focused in the distance. Four figures were approaching me.

And before I could blink again, Kyle had me wrapped in his arms, and I exhaled deeply.

"I got you, baby. I'm here. You're safe now."

21

KYLE

I held her so tightly in my arms, kissed her forehead despite myself. “Are you okay, baby? Did they hurt you?”

Baby. That word hung heavy on my lips. I shouldn’t have called her that—I had no right to call her baby. She was only a mission, one of many hostages I had saved. She wasn’t my woman. I’d told her I wasn’t looking for anything serious. But holding her in my arms made me forget about all the reasons why I’d convinced myself I didn’t want a relationship. Separation, loneliness, stress. Those factors hadn’t changed. But maybe having Sara to come home to would make the struggle of loving someone while I worked a world away worth it.

She buried her face into my chest. “I’m fine now that you’re here. I hurt my ankle running and I’m bruised but they didn’t hurt me to where I couldn’t handle it. Maya?” Her voice was breathy and hopeful. “Did you find her? Is she okay?”

She looked up at me and I brushed back her newly shorter hair, unable to release her. Always so beautiful. “Yes, babe. She’s fine. Thanks to you. You saved her life. You saved both of your lives.”

She shook her head. “No, I didn’t. You did. You found us.”

On closer observation, I saw her face inflamed, and what appeared to be a damn handprint on her cheek. If I could have killed the bastards again I would have. I kissed her lips, knowing I shouldn't, knowing I didn't deserve this kiss. But I would earn the right to kiss her again. And then I'd kiss her any time I wanted. She exhaled when I released her lips. "We only found her because you sacrificed your life. You could've died. She told us about Denise." I spoke of her deceased director so she understood the magnitude of what she'd been through. Then I gave her another kiss, this time on her head, then pulled myself away from her to get back to work.

"Pat, call for air rescue." Pat grabbed his radio and stepped forward a few feet. I had no idea how long it would be until we were airlifted out of here. If the rest of the Teams were still searching for the other women, our command would not jeopardize their mission to get us. We could be here all night guarding Sara, but it didn't matter. She would be safe as long as she was with us.

"Baby, I'm gonna carry you back to the truck. We should get word on rescue by then. Come here." I didn't wait for her to move. Every time the word "baby" came out my mouth she flashed me a pained look. As if I only used it out of guilt or pity. She was wrong.

I lifted her up and cradled her as she wrapped her arms around my neck. Neither of us said another word as I trekked toward the truck. She was so light and looked frail, but underneath all that she was a fighter. I was carrying her the way a man carried his bride, a thought that flashed through my head when I peered down at her slumbering form. Her eyes remained closed as she nuzzled against me, like if she were home. As if she could see me as her man. And I didn't know if I deserved that. But we were not on some tropical honeymoon—we were in the middle of a potential war zone. I remained in the middle, the guys and Cuervo surrounding me, and watched my surroundings.

We were almost back to the truck when Pat approached me from behind. "Good news. The other girls were found in different parts of a nearby village. They are all safe. And Maya and the rest of the Team were picked up as well. Transport will be here soon for all of us. Say goodbye to Sara while you still have time, man."

I stared down at her with such regret. I wasn't ready to say goodbye yet. I kept her tight in my arms, never wanting to let go. Let her sleep as I savored the brief moments I had left.

Once we arrived at the truck, I gave her some water and Vic checked her for injuries. I knew she said she was able to handle it, but I wasn't taking any chances. She was dirty, sore, scratched, and bruised, but she was still as beautiful as ever.

Pat motioned to me and I knew I needed to talk to her before the helicopter approached and prevented us from having any sort of meaningful conversation.

"One helicopter will be sent for you and you will be taken to a hospital. Once you are safely aboard, another will come for us. I'm not going to be allowed to go with you to the hospital because I will need to be debriefed and available for another mission. But, Sara, I want you to know how sorry I am. I *do* want to be with you. I'm sorry I didn't tell you sooner. I thought I knew best but then I almost lost you, and I've been kicking my own ass ever since." A smirk appeared on her soft lips. "I'm going to get in touch with you as soon as I'm allowed to. It could be a while, but I need you to know that I'll be thinking about you. And when I get back home to San Diego, I'm coming to find you. If you'll have me."

"I'd like that, Kyle. I'll be waiting for you."

I knew I shouldn't be kissing a hostage, but I didn't care. The air between us was liable to suffocate me if I didn't kiss her. The rumble of the helicopter shook the earth and told me I only had minutes to say goodbye. My hand grasped the back of her head and I pulled her in for a long kiss. One that would have to last us till we were together again. As our lips met, I was so thankful for the opportunity to kiss her again. She kissed me back, and it felt like the best feeling in the world. She tasted incredible, like sweet freedom. Capturing her bottom lip, I sucked it gently and drew her near, our tongues stroking slow and seductive till her body melted onto mine. It was a crime to release her.

The helicopter hovered over us and I had to say goodbye. Fuck. I reluctantly pulled away and placed her in the arms of the Marine who'd been lowered down to grab her and take her safely inside. She gave a small wave and I winked at her. *My baby.* As Sara melted into the night, I vowed that I would do everything possible to attempt to start a real relationship with her. My fears be damned. I wanted her more. God brought us together for a reason. God spared her life. She was meant for me and I wasn't going to squander another chance to be with her.

22

SARA

SIX WEEKS LATER, SAN DIEGO

I stood in the dressing room at the stadium and took a final look in the long mirror. This was my final game of the season, my rookie season. My life had changed so much since the day I had auditioned a little over a year ago. I'd been kidnapped, held hostage in Afghanistan, risked my life, and been brutalized. And I'd survived. Not many could say that. Nothing about the past year had been easy. I was stronger now, more confident, and mostly not afraid of anything. It was strange how almost dying changed your perspective on things.

Our squad mourned the loss of our director. We'd wept at Denise's funeral, and organized a big fundraiser for her family. I still couldn't believe what had happened to any of us.

Luckily for me, my ankle had only been sprained and not broken, so after rest and physical therapy, I was dancing again. The organization had provided counseling, which helped a lot. It had done wonders for Maya, who still blamed herself for me getting hurt. Which couldn't be farther from the truth.

I spritzed some hairspray into my new bob, courtesy of the shearing of my hair at the hands of Crazy Eyes. When I'd come home, I'd considered having new extensions being placed in, but I realized I wasn't defined by a haircut and decided to proudly rock my short hair. I didn't want to hide behind my hair anymore. It didn't make me who I was, or special. I knew what I was worth, and I finally wanted to go after what I wanted.

And what I wanted was Kyle. He was the calming to the storm of emotions I held inside.

He'd done his best to remain in contact with me, but he had been right, communication was hard with deployed SEAL. There were a few broken satellite calls with the sounds of mortars going off in the background. But despite him calling me baby and making promises when he had rescued me, I hadn't seen him yet, though he had explained to me that he wasn't allowed to tell me when we would return. Operational security. "Soon" was the best I could get out of him. He had sent a dozen roses to my hospital room in Germany and flowers to my home. But I didn't want flowers, I wanted him. Until I saw him again, the possibility of a relationship with him wouldn't seem real to me. Had he just been caught up in the heat of the moment? So thrilled that he had found me? Claimed his prize? Or did he really want a relationship with me? Time would tell.

Insecurity crept up. Maybe he was back stateside and hadn't bothered to contact me. I needed to give him the benefit of the doubt for a little while longer. There was the distinct possibility he was still deployed. I understood and valued his occupation more than ever now. So I'd give him a chance when he returned. One chance, but that was it. If he'd changed his mind or hid his feelings from me, I was through. I couldn't keep doing that to myself.

I straightened in front of the mirror. I didn't have time to stress about him now. Today was Military Appreciation Day, and all the cheerleaders were assigned special uniforms to honor our troops. I'd been assigned Air Force but swapped with Maya and wore the Navy uniform, just in case Kyle was somewhere watching. Old habits were hard to break. And even when I tried not to, he was always heavily on my mind. I missed him.

I pulled up my white boy shorts and tied the top into my bra, heading out to the passageway connecting to the field, poms in hand.

Today we were playing our biggest rival, the Oakland Marauders, which also just happened to be Kyle's former team. When I closed my eyes, I could feel him next to me. Dropping my poms, I stood in line and held a animated expression until Maya whispered, "Thinking about a certain someone, buttercup?" *Kyle, Kyle, Kyle, why was he on my mind so much?* I chastised myself, letting out a slow breath, and prepared myself for the real possibility time didn't in fact heal all things and he had simply moved on. The quiet was deafening. I'd come so far and yet through the silence my feelings hadn't faded, if anything they had intensified. It was true when people said silence was the most powerful scream.

Jan, our interim director, grabbed the megaphone so she could be heard at the end of the line. "All right, ladies. We're on Monday Night Football. Millions of people are watching you. Big smiles."

My mood momentarily changed. I was all smiles. I couldn't believe how blessed I was to be alive. And I couldn't wait to cheer and celebrate the great men and women who served us. I grabbed my poms off the floor and sashayed out to the field and basked in the warmth of the cheering fans.

We lined the entrance as the players ran out and then took our positions around the field in four separate groups. Poms in the air above my head, I fed off of the crowd, riding their energy. Our rescue had been all over the media and though we had been forbidden by the Wildfire organization to do any interviews, the details of our rescue had somehow been leaked to the press.

I smiled at a "Run, Sara, Run!" sign. And while it was sweet, my short time with Kyle taught me one thing—the reward was saving Maya and myself. Kyle didn't advertise his job, and he saved people every day. Despite the reputation of recent SEALs bragging about their kills and raids, Kyle was the ultimate silent operator.

Just as the singer finished her last note, we turned toward the sky. I was eager to see the Blue Angels flyover. I stared toward the sun as the six planes flew in precision formation. I'd always loved seeing them, but today witnessing our nation's military made me so grateful to be an American. The crowd roared in heavy cheering.

"And now, a special treat. The Navy Leapfrogs."

A helicopter hovered overhead, and for a brief moment I flashed back to being rescued, and Kyle holding me in his arms and handing me off to a Marine. Like angels from the sky, two black and yellow parachutes opened and two men came floating down carrying Navy flags. The audience roared as they executed a perfect landing.

My poms were still in the air when I noticed that one of the Leapfrogs was heading right toward my section.

My breath hitched. And I brought a hand to my chest as tears started to form. It was Kyle.

My chest rose and fell, my breathing galloping like a wild horse, and I broke my formation, not caring whether or not I would get in trouble, and ran toward him. He sprinted across the field and before I knew it, he had scooped me up into his arms. Our lips met and the electricity exploded between us. Or maybe those bright flashes were the cameras goin

"I can't believe you're here! That was quite an entrance."

"I had to pull some strings to swap with the guy who normally does this. But seeing you was worth it." He smirked. "Baby. Let me look at you." He pulled back, his teeth digging into his button lip. "Wow. You look amazing. I just wanted to see you in that Navy pinup uniform. I had a feeling you'd be wearing it. Of course, it will look better on my floor." My cheeks flushed bright pink. He was what I thought about when I was *alone*. "I missed you, babe. I'm back. And I can't wait to see you do your thing. I'm gonna watch you dance for me up in the box with some of my old teammates. But when this game is over, I'm taking you home. In fact, you're never going home alone again."

23

KYLE

It was good to be back home. We'd returned a week ago but I had been so busy debriefing my commander and readjusting to civilian life, I was anxious. I needed to be with my girl. But I didn't want to see Sara until I could make her my top priority. My only priority. Until the only thing I saw, breathed, and tasted was her.

Plus I wanted to arrive in style. I was bringing the romance. She deserved it.

I relaxed in the box seat and for a moment, I was back in my old life. A baller. Surrounded by my former football friends. I dined on catered lobster and sipped Cristal. And while I appreciated the finer things in life, it didn't have the same effect. Don't get me wrong, it was great. Just different.

My old buddy, JaMarcus King, eased up next to me. Always good to see one of my boys. "Hey, T.K. Man, good to see you."

"You too, man. How you been?"

JaMarcus pointed to his knee. "Good, bro. Good. My knee is busted but doc says I should be able to play next season. How 'bout you? Ever think of coming back?"

I shook my head. "Nope. Not for me."

He bit his lip and leaned in close. "Hey, you never told me. Why did you leave? I mean the truth."

I exhaled. I had held this truth to my chest for years. My fellow frogmen didn't even know the reason. But after vowing to start new with Sara, I decided to break my silence. JaMarcus had always been a good friend. A true friend. "Remember that night? In Dallas? With those girls?"

He nodded. "How could I forget? Damn those bitches."

Damn those bitches indeed. JaMarcus knew exactly what I meant. I didn't need to go into the details. But I planned to bare my soul to Sara.

But for now, I would enjoy a vacation to my past. I stared down at the field and watched my girl light up the field. She was on fire, completely magnetic. When the cameras focused on her smile and she lit up the 160-foot screen, I knew I was the luckiest man alive.

24

SARA

I changed out of my uniform. My nerves rattled. I'd been anticipating my reunion with Kyle for well over six weeks. But I hadn't been prepared to see him today. On any given day, the time sped by or moved slower than molasses. I was ready then I wasn't. I just wanted everything to be perfect. Finally enjoy this. Enjoy us.

Maya spritzed me with perfume. "Look, I want you to be happy. Maybe I was wrong about Kyle. Just make sure he treats you right or he'll have me to deal with me." There was the Maya I knew.

"Maybe?"

I laughed and she hugged me. "Okay, I couldn't have been more wrong. I love you, Sara. You saved my life. You're my family. I want to see you happy. You deserve it."

Her eyes watered and I pulled back. "Don't make me cry. I just touched up my makeup. Horror show is not exactly the look I'm going for."

She threw her head back and laughed. "I love you. Take care of yourself." Bringing her hand to her chin in fake wonderment, she added, "See you in what? A week? I'll know it's you by the penguin waddle."

"Oh my god. Stop." She winked at me before walking backward in the opposite direction, heading to meet up with the other girls. As we separated, I walked out of the locker room and made a beeline to my right. I didn't make it far. Kyle was standing there across the hall in the corner holding a dozen roses. He had shed his parachute gear and uniform and looked so handsome in a fitted designer suit. Too handsome. He took my breath away.

"Hey, beautiful."

"Hi. I still can't believe you're here," I intoned softly, inching closer to him.

He put his arm around me and led me outside. Even though it was January, San Diego was still warm in the evening. A stretch limo awaited us and suddenly I became overcome with emotions. It was foreign to see him go all out.

He kissed the side of my neck, causing goose bumps to travel across my skin, then opened the door, stretching out his hand so I'd go in first. The limo driver promptly set off and Kyle and I wasted no time and necked like two teenagers. I'd never get enough of him. His scent. His touch. They intoxicated me.

"I don't roll like this anymore. But tonight is a special occasion."

"Oh really? What is that?" I teased. All I really needed was him.

"Our first date."

I couldn't help it. I laughed. We'd had sex twice, once was a hot one-night stand, next time was on a war bunker. We were kind of doing this backward. Then he'd saved me from terrorists. Yep. Most definitely backward.

But that didn't change the fact that we didn't really know each other at all. I had strong feelings for a man I knew only on the surface. We were bound together by these incredible experiences, but did we have enough in common to build a future?

I'd find out tonight.

25

KYLE

I never got nervous, never. Not before a mission, not before a football game, not even during drown proofing at BUD/S. But I had to admit, Sara made me nervous.

Tonight, I would spoil her. The limo dropped us off at the Grand Del Mar hotel and we walked into the upscale French restaurant, Addison. I was more of a steak and potatoes guy, but this place was supposedly the best and Sara deserved the best.

Well, at least this place was romantic. The lighting was dim, and we were escorted to a huge private booth near the blazing fire. I hadn't done this romance stuff in so long, my hands grew clammy as we sat. I wiped them on my pants. We ordered the chef's twelve-course tasting menu and a sommelier picked our wine pairings.

As we indulged in oysters and champagne, I took Sara's hand. If I was going to be honest, now was as good a time as any.

"Look, I wanted to tell you something. Something I never tell anyone."

Her eyes brightened. "What?"

"Why I stopped playing ball."

"I'm dying to know. But you don't have to tell me, Kyle. It's apparent it's hard for you to talk about it if you've kept it to yourself for this long."

She stared at me through long, fluttering lashes. I exhaled. The words that I'd held back. I was going to speak my truth. She squeezed my hands, signaling it was all going to be okay. And I cleared my throat.

"After playing for a few years, I was getting tired of the scene. But, I'll be honest, I was addicted to the lifestyle. When I told my then girlfriend I was considering leaving football, she dumped me. She wanted to be a football wife."

Sara squeezed my hand again and I couldn't help staring at the way the candlelight illuminated her chest. Every time she took a breath it rose like what I said hung on a knife's edge. "That's horrible, Kyle. She obviously wasn't right for you."

"No, she wasn't. I see that now. But, it really got to me then. I felt that everyone around me was just after my money. No one liked me, the true me. But, for a while, I was just pissed and started acting out. It all blew up one night. My buddy JaMarcus and I had only one night left in Dallas. After a year on the road, it had turned into the same thing every night. Different state, different girl. We'd met two girls in the bar that night. They didn't seem like typical groupies, not that we would've cared if they were. So we took them up to our suite. I started to kiss one of the girls and she was super aggressive and handed me a condom. Now, I always had my own stash, but she insisted. She was hot and I was drunk so I tossed caution to the wind and rolled the condom on, and there at the tip was a hole. A fucking hole. She had poked a hole in the condom. How sick is that? I pulled up my pants and told her to get out. To say I was mad was an understatement. But I had a revelation that night. I was on the wrong path. I used people just as much as they used me. I was a damn opportunist with a god complex. I didn't even recognize myself anymore. When I did, I felt alone. People's loyalty ended the minute the benefits stopped. The sex wasn't the *only* thing that was dirty. And I should have known better. That's the thing about being shallow—it doesn't take long to be emptied and sink to the bottom. So I chose to walk away and find my own peace. Because that person, yeah, that person wasn't me."

"But you made a change. You left and joined the Navy."

"Yes, I joined the Navy to be a SEAL. But honestly, I didn't change my personal life. Being a SEAL didn't change that—just as many women want to be fucked by a SEAL as they want to be fucked by a baller. Now I was honest about my intentions up front. People could take it or leave it. Women every night, frog hogs, and groupies, I was just a notch on their belts. Not saying I was any better, but at least I wasn't a liar or a user. They'd been warned. I figured as long as I served my country and devoted my life for others, I'd be absolved of the shitty things I did on my downtime. Basically, I lied to myself and didn't give a fuck. Until I met you." She stayed quiet and stared at me, appearing conflicted. Fuck it. Might as well finish. "I'm not going to lie to you. Or sugarcoat things to sound pretty. At first, I thought you were no different than the rest. I told you I played professionally, and you went home with me. The whole situation reminded me of going to the hotel with the chick from Dallas, only I was controlling the situation." She let go of my hand, and it was like being thrown into freezing water. "I have to finish, Sara." She motioned for me to continue but kept her hands on the table. And it took all I had not to reach across the table and demand she place her hands back on mine. She needed to understand she was part of me now.

I'm so sorry, baby.

"Speak, Kyle." So I did.

"Still, I had no intention of calling you. Ever. Even if I hadn't deployed. But you seemed so open and honest. The following week I told myself I was doing the right thing. If you were as amazing as you seemed, then getting mixed with me was a bad idea. I was doing you a favor. Then seeing you in Afghanistan was a total shock. I knew I couldn't stay away from you. On our night together on the bunker, I started to feel something, but I was so stuck in my way of life. It was selfish of me to get involved with you again when I didn't have my head on straight. And I almost told you before you left, but I punked out. But I'm telling you, Sara, when they took you..." I paused, trying to lock down my anger, "I mean it. I lost it. I had to find you. I don't think I ever would've recovered if I had lost you. Please." I covered her smaller hands with mine. "That feeling of being used is something I unfairly inflicted on you, even when you showed me you were kind. You trusted me and I failed you. And for that I'm sorry. It's hard to trust people when all you've ever gotten was burned. But that's no excuse. And that's not how I should have treated someone I had fallen in love with." Her lips trembled, and she closed her eyes. "Sara?" And that's when I saw it. She looked like she was fighting back tears. And I was done hurting her.

I slid next to her. My fucking heart hurt seeing her like this. "Baby, look at me, please." Cupping her face, I brought it up to meet mine. I was ready to apologize until I was blue in the face. Whatever it took to have her look at me again on her own free will. But before I had a chance to utter another word her eyes opened and she kissed me. Feel-it-in-my-bones kissed me. My groin hurt as her warm mouth pressed against mine and she sank her tongue in my mouth. I could feel her everywhere, and I grew harder. Cornering her in the booth, I gave zero fucks that we were out in public. She worked my mouth hungrily and I couldn't get enough. I couldn't explain it. Had no idea why she was kissing me, and I wasn't going to question it.

I let go of her face, bracing one hand on the table and the other behind her head, pulling her in and kissed her back, swallowed her moans, drank in her lips, and willed time to stop because I never wanted this moment to end. When she pulled back from my lips, her breath uneven, I started to worry she'd regretted it.

"I-I'm not upset. I'm relieved," she panted. Swallowing, she spoke more clearly. "I had the same reservations. I just fell faster than you did. I've known for some time now I fell in love with you. I just didn't say anything because I was afraid you didn't feel the same. You hide your emotions better than anyone I know. When you were being honest about our beginning, it just opened a fresh wound for me. The more you spoke, the more uncomfortable you seem to get, and I started to think you brought me here to relieve your conscience and back out on what you'd said."

My eyes hooded, and I grew mad at myself. I'd put that doubt in her.

"No." I lightly kissed her lips. "I want you. I need you. All of you, all the time. I'll be faithful to you. Come home from deployments only to you. This," I pointed at her chest, "I'm never letting it go."

She leaned in and gave me a soft kiss on the lips then worked her way to my neck, kissing her way up to my ear. "Kyle… Let's get out of here."

I turned and signaled to the waiter. "Check please!"

26

SARA

He made me wait. Prolonged being devoured by him. Initially I'd felt like pouting. Not having my hands all over him was cruel. But I was beginning to see why he'd done it. The view was breathtaking. And it felt good to be okay with just being silent with him. We were comfortable with each other. We strolled hand in hand across the lavish grounds of the resort. Walking under the moonlight on this night reminded me of the first night I went home with Kyle. I'd never in my wildest imagination would've believed that six months later we would be dating after falling in love a world away.

My heels clicked on the cobblestones that paved the elaborate grounds as Kyle led me into the lobby of resort. This place was spectacular. A huge crystal chandelier hung from the ceiling and the scents of pine cones and nutmeg filled the air. A gigantic Christmas tree still graced the center of the room.

My pulsed picked up when Kyle checked in and the bellhop led us to our room. Or shall I say suite. There were rose petals on the heart-shaped bed and a fresh bottle of Cristal on the rocks. Why was he spending so much money on me?

My fingers tingled. Was I nervous? I'd already had sex with

this man twice before, but for some reason I felt like this time would be very different.

He'd set the mood. This would be the first time we made love.

I had barely turned to face him when Kyle had already pulled me back into his arms. He brushed my hair off my neck and planted a soft kiss there, then on my chest, taking a moment to inhale me. Made sure I was real. I was very real. And this was happening. My hand grasped at the nape of his neck. His mouth turned up to mine and our lips met. Our one chaste kiss turned deeper and harder as the intensity built between us.

Our breaths picked up speed and he reached a hand around my back and unzipped my dress in a single motion, its fabric pooling on the floor. My mind went fuzzy, not knowing where to put my own hands. One heady grasp of my chin as he cupped it to kiss my lips and I snapped out of it and went to work on the buttons of his shirt, desperate to see his incredible chest underneath. I pushed the shirt off him and stopped to pause and just stared.

His eyes sparkled. He was staring right back at me, as I stood before him in nothing but my black lace bra, thong, and heels. "You're so beautiful, baby. Come here. Let me worship you."

Stepping closer, he slowly guided a hand over my body, pausing at the center of my breasts and placed a single open-mouthed kiss on my skin before straightening and tracing the hand down the curve of my back until it landed on my ass. One smack. Two. Swallowing hard, I stared into his eyes and he gave me a smile before he took his other hand and stroked my nipples through my bra. His left hand remained on my bottom as he rubbed the tantalizing burn away. I let out a moan and this only caused him to smirk wickedly, and with one sweep he raised the hand and undid my bra. My exposed skin was on fire.

My hands undid the belt on his pants and they dropped to the ground. He stood in his boxer briefs and my eyes couldn't help but focus on his bulge. I was so ready for him, but he continued to tease me. This was sweet torture.

He placed me sitting on the bed and knelt in front of me. Then brought his mouth to my right breast and took my nipple between his teeth and he lightly grazed it. This slow burn was pure torment for me. I'd been wanting him for so long, imagining our reunion—this was almost unbearable. I could hardly believe we were back together, starting our life together. The man in front of me loved me.

"You look like an angel. Damn, Sara." And this was heaven.

He slowly pulled my panties down as he kissed his way down my inner legs. His teasing was growing more and more torturous as his lips made their way back up my legs. He paused and smirked, giving me small bites across my thighs, before kissing the final stretch to the top and taking a long lap of his tongue straight up my center.

"Oh, that feels amazing." I arched back.

"You taste incredible, baby." I bit my lip, wanting him to continue.

He licked and licked, first around the edges then focusing on my clit, and I shuddered. His tongue felt divine. I was so wet, so ready for him, I sat back up and pulled his head up. Tingles spread throughout my body, liquid fire traveling in my veins. I wanted my mouth on him. Craved tasting him. I wanted to drop to my knees and give him the same incredible pleasure he had just given me.

But he quickly took control, producing an enormous grin and wagging a finger at me. Tease. The anticipation was killing me. He pulled out a condom, rolled it on his thick cock, and pressed me back on the bed.

My eyes closed. "Please, Kyle."

"Look at me, I want you to look at me, Sara."

He pressed into me, ever so gradually, inch by inch as I gasped. His expression darkened as he slammed into me. "Oh, God."

Once he was deeply inside of me, I grasped his ass, never wanting to be apart from him again. But he wasn't moving. "Do you need me to move?" God, yes. To prove his point, he rotated his hips, his dick licking my walls. The man was pure evil but in the best possible way.

I nodded franticly. "Say it, Sara."

"Yes!" I purred. He cradled my face and kissed me as he pumped, deeper and deeper, faster until I was thrashing on the bed. I would never get enough of him. He broke from my mouth and chuckled and went faster, deeper.

I was so close to coming and I knew Kyle could sense it but he slowed the pace as my orgasm built deep inside me. No! He took me by surprise when he brought a hand down and pressed the pad of his thumb on my clit. "I'm willing to bet you want me to move this as well?"

I was ready to explode and grew impatient. Bringing my own hand down, I set it over his. "Either you move or I will," I threatened on a hurried breath.

"Actually, I like that idea. Pleasure yourself," he teased, then shocked me by sinking in me. My fingers worked at the same speed as his cock was pleasuring me. Pulse after pulse of pleasure rippled through my body as he pounded me hard one last time and I came so fucking hard I almost blacked out. My legs twitched and I basked in the love I saw in his eyes.

He pulled out of me and I dropped my hand, which felt numb and tingly now. And he rolled onto his back and held me in his arms, so tightly, our wet bodies plastered together.

"I love you, Sara."

"I love you, too."

I had a feeling that from that night on, if he was in the country, we would never spend a night apart again. We lay back and gasped, air expelling from our lungs as we tried to catch our breaths.

"Welcome home, Kyle."

EPILOGUE

NEXT DECEMBER, CAMP RHINO, AFGHANISTAN

Pat, Vic, and I stood awaiting the USO tour plane. A year ago, I stood at this same place, no idea my life would change when that same plane landed.

Pat punched my arm. "You sure?"

"Never been surer about anything in my life," I answered confidently.

I clutched the ring in my right pocket. Even though I still had substantial wealth left over from my football days, I never flaunted it. And besides that one amazing night back in San Diego, I'd never spent recklessly.

But I broke that rule when it came to her ring.

I'd called a jeweler I knew back in my ball days and he helped me design a custom ring. A five-carat, flawless stunner. It was perfect, just like Sara.

Our year had gone smoother than I'd expected it to. We rarely argued, she was patient and didn't complain about the time I spent away from her at training or deployments. I had to give it to her. I was the one that moaned and groaned on occasion about our time apart. I missed her so fucking much. She'd moved into my place in August and we'd followed into a rhythm.

But I'd been lying to her. I kept telling her I didn't want to get married. Not until I was out of the Teams. She hadn't nagged me, but clearly made her feelings known that she wanted to get married.

Last year she'd shocked the hell out of me and it was time I returned the favor.

The plane touched down and Sara was the first off. No surprise there. We hadn't seen each other in three months. She ran into my arms and I swung her around.

On cue, Maya began to film the moment. I'd contacted her a week ago. I'd been a bit worried that she'd spill my secret, but she swore that she would keep quiet.

Sara's eyes grew to the size of saucers when I set her back down and knelt in front of her, taking her hand in mine.

"Sara," I began.

Before I could say the next word, she screamed. "Oh my god, Kyle. Oh my god!"

I opened the box. "You saved me. I love you so much. Baby, will you marry me?"

"Yes! Oh my god, yes!" she squealed, and I placed the ring on her finger.

No sooner had I done that when Maya grabbed Sara's hand out of mine. "Damn, look at that rock. Nicely done, Kyle. Congrats, Sara."

I cleared my throat. "Uh, Maya?"

"Sorry, I got a little happy. I'm still recording though. I zoomed in on that baby." Laughing, I focused my attention back on Sara. She was all smiles. And surprised. Mission accomplished.

"I didn't think you wanted to get married! You kept saying how happy you were with the way things were. What changed your mind?"

"You, baby. You."

The other girls swarmed her and she showed off her ring.

I pulled her away, cupping her face and kissing those lips I couldn't get enough of. After I was satisfied with the kiss since she looked drunk with anticipation of what the kiss would lead to, I took her hand and pulled her with me as I walked backward. "Where are we going?"

"To my barracks room. You're not getting out of my sight this time."

STAY TUNED FOR INFALLIBLE

TRIDENT CODE #3

Vic's Story

Coming Summer 2017

AUTHOR'S NOTE

Thank you for reading my book.
If you liked it, would you please consider leaving a review?
Invaluable
For the latest updates, release, and giveaways, subscribe to
***Alana's newsletter*.**
For all her available books, check out Alana's ***website*** or
Facebook page.

INFALLIBLE

TRIDENT CODE #3

I'll be honest with you—I'm not perfect. Sure, I live my life by the code. Honor, integrity, loyalty. I'm a lover, I'm a fighter. There's a line we say in BUD/S: Clarity is in the eyes, love is in the heart, and fear is in the mind. I'm a mother fucking Navy SEAL—I'm invincible, invaluable, infallible. But behind all the machismo and hype, I'm a simple man . . . all I really want is a woman to claim as mine.

A summer affair—washed away with the ebb and flow of the tides. I met her on dog beach—flowing red hair, full breasts, hypnotic scent. After we made love in the sand, I pretended that she was mine forever—that she would be faithful while I was gone, supportive of my career, loving to my daughter.

But we'd built our relationship on lies—I'd never told her I was a SEAL, she'd kept her past hidden from me. She'd had a man, if you could call him that. He was cruel, abusive, controlling. She'd fled, determined to start a new life, but he'd found her, and would stop at nothing to get her back—dead or alive.

But he didn't count on meeting me. I am the person who everyone knows will lay down my life for someone else. Failure is not an option. I lived by the sword, would die by the sword. I may not be perfect, but I am perfect for her.

ALSO BY ALANA ALBERTSON

Want more romance?

Love Navy SEALS?

Meet Pat! I had one chance to put on the cape and be her hero. ***Invincible***

Meet Kyle! I'll never win MVP, never get a championship ring, but some heroes don't play games. ***Invaluable***

Meet Grant! She wants to get wild? I will fulfill her every fantasy. ***Conceit, Chronic, Crazed, Carnal, Crave, Consume, Covet***

Meet Shane! I'm America's cockiest badass. ***Badass*** (co-written with ***Linda Barlow***)

Love Marines?

Meet Grady! With tattooed arms sculpted from carrying M-16s, this bad boy has girls begging from sea to shining sea to get a piece of his action. ***Beast***

Meet Bret! He was a real man—muscles sculpted from carrying weapons, not from practicing pilates. ***Grunt***

Love demons?

Who's haunting America's favorite ballet? ***Snow Queen***

ACKNOWLEDGMENTS

I WOULD LIKE TO THANK my husband, Roger for supporting all my dreams. Thank you for being such a wonderful husband to me and the best daddy to our sons. For watching the boys while I write. For keeping me caffeinated and fed during late night writing sessions. I love you.

To Nicole Blanchard. I would've quit this book 1000 times if it wasn't for you. Thank you for not allowing me to give up.

I would like to thank my editor, Marilyn Medina for breaking through the block on this book. Your astute edits saved this book!

To Indie Sage Promotions for handling all the promotion for the book.

To all the fans who have written me about Invaluable and asked about Kyle's story. Thank you for all your support

ABOUT THE AUTHOR

ALANA ALBERTSON IS the former President of Romance Writers of America's Contemporary Romance Chapter. She holds a M.Ed. from Harvard and a BA in English from Stanford. A recovering professional ballroom dancer, she lives in San Diego, California, with her husband, two young sons, and five dogs. When she's not saving dogs from high kill shelters through her rescue Pugs N Roses, she can be found watching episodes of House Hunters, Homeland, or Dallas Cowboys Cheerleaders: Making the Team.

For more information:

www.alanaalbertson.com
alana@alanaalbertson.com